Bumpy Ride Ahead!

Mattie & Mark Miller · Double Trouble

WANDA E. BRUNSTETTER

BARBOUR PUBLISHING

Published by Barbour Publishing, Inc., P.O. Box 719, Uhrichsville, Ohio 44683, www.barbourbooks.com

Our mission is to publish and distribute inspirational products offering exceptional value and biblical encouragement to the masses.

Member of the
Evangelical Christian
Publishers Association

Printed in the United States of America.
Dickinson Press, Inc., Grand Rapids, MI 49512; September 2012; D10003513

DEDICATION

To Helen Ballard and the children in her class
at the school I've visited in Walnut Creek, Ohio.

GLOSSARY

absatz—stop
ach—oh
achtsam—careful
appeditlich—delicious
baremlich—terrible
bickel—pickle
bletsching—spanking
blumme—flowers
bopp—doll
boppli—baby
bruder—brother
buch—book
daed—dad
danki—thanks
daremlich—dizzy
dumm—dumb
eegesinnisch—selfish
faahre—ride
gaul—horse
gern—nap
glicker—marble
grank—sick
gut—good

hund–dog
hundli–puppy
hungerich–hungry
hunnskop–dog's head
jah–yes
katz–cat
keffer–bugs
kichlin–cookies
kinner–children
Kumme, schnell!–Come, quickly!
leinduch–sheets
maedel–girl
mamm–mom
mann–man
niesse–sneeze
schnee–snow
Sei net so eegesinnisch!–Don't be so selfish!
walnuss–walnut
wasser–water
Wie geht's?–How are you?
yung bu–young boy

CONTENTS

CHAPTER 1

A Troublesome Day

"Sure wish we could do somethin' fun today," nine-year-old Mark Miller complained to his twin sister, Mattie, as they headed down the driveway toward their parents' roadside stand. "Selling fruits and vegetables from our garden is just plain boring—especially now, since it's supposed to be nice out today."

"I agree," Mattie said, swatting at a bug that had landed on her arm. "We're in school all week and don't have much time to play when we get home. Because it's Saturday and already warm outside, I was hoping I could visit my friend Stella Schrock."

School had started a few weeks ago, and even though summer was officially over, there was no sign that the mild weather was going away just yet. In a few weeks they'd probably be wearing jackets, but not today. It was warm and comfortable, and the humidity was low. Although a few pesky insects were still around, they'd be gone in a few short weeks.

This morning the blue, cloudless sky made the land-scape look so pretty. Mattie didn't think it was fair that she and Mark were stuck watching their roadside stand today.

"I was hoping I could go fishin' today." Mark took a seat on one of the stools behind the wooden stand and folded his arms.

"Maybe we'll sell everything really quick. Then we can do whatever we want for the rest of the day," Mattie said with a hopeful smile as she watched a brownish-orange butterfly flit past and hover near some flowering bushes that were close to the stand. "Did ya see that pretty butterfly, Mark?"

Mark looked where Mattie was pointing. "Oh, that's a Great Spangled Fritillary."

"A Frita-what?" Mattie scrunched up her nose. "Are we talkin' about the same thing?"

"I was talkin' about the butterfly. Isn't that what you were referring to—about how pretty it was?" Mark answered.

Mattie nodded, thinking to herself, *Here we go again with the big words.*

"Well, that butterfly is a Great Spangled Fritillary, and it's common in our state of Ohio. It can be seen from June until October, and it thrives in woods, fields, and gardens. And," Mark added, "these butterflies lay their eggs on violets."

"Wow, you sure know a lot about this butterfly!"

"That's 'cause I like to read about things." Changing to a new topic, Mark pointed to the stack of pumpkins on the ground to the right of the stand. "Do ya really think we're gonna sell all those?"

Mattie shrugged. "We'd have a lot more if we hadn't given some of our pumpkins to our cousins Harold and Mary to sell at their stand."

"Well, at least Mom and Dad said we could keep the money we make from all the pumpkins we sell."

"That's true, but we also have potatoes, apples, beets, pears, and some of Mom's *kichlin* and homemade bread for sale. 'Course, any money we make from that will go to Mom and Dad."

Mark looked at the tray full of goodies Mom had brought out earlier and licked his lips. "Those peanut butter kichlin sure look *appeditlich*, don't they? I could eat a few of 'em right now."

Mattie nodded. "The cookies do look delicious, but you'd better not eat any 'cause Mom's kichlin usually sell really well."

"Wish we could keep every bit of the money we make here today," Mark said. "I'd like to buy a new yo-yo and some other fun things."

Mattie sighed and leaned her elbows on the edge of the wooden surface. "Mom made the baked goods and Dad grew the produce, so it's only fair that they should get most of the money."

Mark motioned to a car that had just pulled up near the stand. "Wow, now that was quick! Looks like our first customer is already here."

Mattie smiled. "That's good. I hope they buy lots of things."

A tall woman with short brown hair and a young blond-haired girl, who looked to be about Mattie's age, got out of the car and approached the stand. "We need two nice big pumpkins," the woman said, opening her purse and removing a leather wallet.

Mattie motioned to the pumpkins sitting on the

ground, sure that the woman would want to buy a few. "We have them in all shapes and sizes."

While the woman looked at the pumpkins, the girl leaned her elbows on the edge of the stand and stared at Mattie. "My name's Joyce. What's yours?"

"Mattie."

"How old are you?" she asked, blinking her blue eyes rapidly.

"My brother and I are both nine years old." Mattie motioned to Mark. "We're twins, and his name is Mark."

Joyce looked at Mark then back at Mattie. "You do sort of look alike—same red hair, same blue eyes."

"But we're different as day and night," Mark was quick to say. He stepped off the stool, and when he bent down to pick up an odd-shaped rock near the toe of his boot, his straw hat fell off. This caused his thick red hair to stand straight up.

Mattie tried not to giggle, so she focused on the rock in her brother's hand instead of his funny-looking hair. Since Mark liked to collect rocks of all sizes and shapes, Mattie figured he would probably add this one to his collection.

"You have big ears, and your hair looks funny." Joyce snickered as she stared at Mark.

"Joyce! You apologize right now. That was not nice," the girl's mother scolded.

"I'm sorry," Joyce said, but she didn't sound very sincere.

"That's okay," Mark answered, and then he walked away from the impolite little girl.

"Where's your mother?" Joyce asked, looking back at Mattie with a strange expression.

"She's up at the house baking more pies and bread for us to sell." Mattie pointed to the baked goods sitting on the counter. "Don't they look good?"

Joyce's blue eyes widened. "You mean, your mother sent you and your brother out here by yourselves?" she asked, ignoring Mattie's question.

"That's right. Everyone in our family, except for our little sister and brother, takes a turn selling things here at the stand." Mattie glanced over toward where Mark had been standing, but he wasn't there. He had wandered away, looking for more rocks, no doubt.

Mark shouldn't leave me here to talk to this girl by myself, Mattie thought. *He's being selfish right now.*

Joyce pointed to the black bonnet on Mattie's head. "How come you're wearing a hat and long dress?"

"Because I'm Amish, and this is how we dress," Mattie explained, wondering what the curious girl's next question might be.

Joyce opened her mouth, like she might say something more, but the woman spoke first. "I didn't see any pumpkins I like," she said, rising to her feet and putting her wallet away. "I'm sorry, but none of them are big enough."

"Oh, I see." Mattie couldn't help feeling a bit disappointed. "Is there anything else you'd like?" she asked. "We have lots of other fruits and vegetables for sale, and plenty of baked goods, too."

The woman slowly shook her head. "All I need are some pumpkins right now."

"Our cousins down the road have pumpkins for sale," Mark said, moving back to the stand.

"Why, thank you," the woman said, smiling. "I believe

we'll check that out." She paused a moment and then quickly added, "I'm sorry I couldn't find the right size pumpkins I need, but you've been most helpful referring us to your cousins."

"You're welcome," Mark said.

Mattie waited until the woman and her daughter got into their car, then she turned to Mark and said, "Why'd you tell her about the pumpkins we gave Harold and Mary to sell at their stand?"

" 'Cause she didn't like our pumpkins and wanted somethin' else." Mark gave Mattie's arm a quick jab. "Don't worry about it. I'm sure we'll sell some of our pumpkins, and I bet it'll be soon."

Mattie hoped Mark was right, but she had a funny feeling this might not be a good day.

✿

An hour went by, and not one single customer came. Mark was bored and tired of sitting and waiting. Mattie seemed fine with it, though. She had her nose in a book.

Mark nudged Mattie's arm, and when she pulled it away, her elbow banged the wooden counter. "Want to go play in that?" he asked, pointing to the mound of leaves their brother Russell had raked into a pile the day before.

Mattie shook her head. "Ouch!"

"What's wrong?"

"I got a splinter in my elbow," she said.

"Want me to see if I can get it out?"

"That's okay. I can manage." Mattie picked at the place where the splinter stabbed her skin. "There—it's out now."

"That's good. Now do you wanna play a game?"

"Huh-uh," she replied. "And please don't jab me again. It was your fault I got that nasty old splinter."

"It wouldn't have happened if you hadn't jerked away when I bumped your arm." Mark reached over and tickled Mattie under the chin. "Aw, come on, let's play a game; it'll be fun."

Mattie shook her head so hard that the ribbon ties connected to her bonnet swished around her face. "Whenever I play one of your silly games, it usually means some kind of trouble for me."

"This game won't cause you any trouble—I promise," Mark said.

"I don't care. I'm not gonna play. I'm gonna sit here and read my *buch* until another customer shows up."

"Suit yourself." Mark hurried off, stopping in front of the huge pile of leaves. Then he reached into his pants' pocket and took out a large blue marble. Grandpa Troyer had given the marble to Mark last summer, and it was the biggest in his collection.

Mark stepped into the pile of leaves and tossed the marble into the air, watching as it dropped. Then he reached into the leaves, felt around, and grabbed the marble out.

This is so easy, he thought. *I figured it'd be harder to find the marble, but it's not.*

Mark tossed the marble into the air again, let it drop, dug into the leaves, and pulled the marble out. "Want to see what I can do with my marble?" he called to Mattie.

Still showing no interest, Mattie shook her head. "Someone has to watch the stand."

Mark shrugged and kept tossing the marble and then

picking it up. He'd just thrown it into the air once more when—*woof! woof!*—a big black shaggy dog came out of nowhere, barking loudly and wagging its tail. The mutt wore no collar, and its fur was matted with briars. Mark was pretty sure it must be a stray.

"Get away from here!" Mattie shouted when the dog bumped into the stand. "Mark, *kumme, schnell!*"

Mark figured he'd better go quickly like Mattie had asked, or the dog might knock something over and make a mess of things.

He hurried back to the stand, for the moment forgetting about his marble. "Get away from here you troublesome *hund*!" he hollered, waving his hands.

Woof! Woof! The dog's long pink tongue hung out of the side of his mouth as he raced back and forth, circled the stand, and came to a halt in front of the basket of apples. Hunkered down on his front legs and watching the twins as if wanting them to play, the mutt barked again. *Woof! Woof! Woof!*

Mark made a lunge for the dog but missed. The critter stuck his snout into the basket, snatched an apple in his mouth, and darted away.

Mark started after the dog until Mattie shouted, "Just let him go, Mark! He's got what he wants, and we sure don't want the apple back now that it's been in the hund's slobbery mouth."

Mark stopped running and returned to the stand. "You were right, Mattie. It doesn't look like we're gonna make any money today," he said with a frown.

"The day's not over yet. Maybe someone will come along soon," Mattie said with a hopeful-looking smile.

Mark's stomach rumbled. "I'm *hungerich*. Think I'm gonna eat one of Mom's kichlin."

Mattie shook her head. "You'd better not. Mom said she'd bring us something to eat when it's time for lunch, and if we start eating cookies there won't be any left to sell."

"I don't care. We haven't sold one single thing all morning, and I doubt that we will."

Mattie tipped her head and looked toward the road. "I hear a horse and buggy coming. Maybe the driver will stop at our stand."

Mark listened to the steady *clip-clop*, *clip-clop* of the horse's hooves. A few minutes later, a horse and black box-shaped buggy pulled up near the stand. Mark recognized the elderly driver and his wife—Elam and Martha Fisher. Elam held the reins while Martha climbed out of the buggy. "Do you have any carrots?" she asked, smiling at the twins.

Mark shook his head. "All we have for sale is what's sitting out."

"That's too bad. I really need some carrots for the vegetable soup I'm planning to make later today," Martha said.

Mattie spoke up. "Our cousins down the road have a stand, and they might have some carrots."

Martha smiled. "*Danki.* We'll go there now and check it out." She turned and climbed back into the buggy.

Mark looked at Mattie and frowned. "Looks like our cousins are gonna make all the money today 'cause we sure aren't making any. Think I'll go back to the pile of leaves and look for the marble I dropped there."

Mattie's eyebrows shot straight up. "How are you gonna find it in all those leaves?"

"It's simple. I saw where I dropped it, so I'll just reach inside and pick it up, just like I did a couple of times before. It's a fun game. You really oughta come and watch."

"Now this I've gotta see." Mattie followed Mark to the pile of leaves and stood watching as he dug around for the marble.

Mark's forehead wrinkled as he frowned. "That's really strange. I'm sure I dropped it right here," he said, scooping out some of the leaves and peering into the hole.

Woof! Woof! The big black dog that had taken the apple came running down the road and headed straight for the stand again. Before Mark or Mattie could do a thing, the bouncing dog knocked the tray of cookies on the ground and gobbled them all up, leaving only the crumbs clinging to his whiskers.

Mattie hollered, and just as Mark was about to chase after the dog, the critter leaped into the air and landed in the pile of leaves with a thud! Then he stuck his nose in the leaves and grunted as he pushed them all around. The next thing Mark knew, the dog had scattered the leaves everywhere and trampled the ground.

"Oh no!" Mattie cried. "That hund's not only eaten Mom's kichlin, but he's made a big mess, and now those leaves will have to be raked all over again."

Mark got down on his hands and knees, hoping to locate his marble, but it was nowhere to be found. "My *glicker* is gone, and I'll probably never get it back. Wish I'd never gotten out of bed this morning!" he muttered.

"Calm down, Mark," Mattie said. "You're gettin' yourself all worked up."

"That's easy for you to say. You didn't lose something

special to you in that pile of leaves."

"If the marble was so special, then you should have been more careful with it. You shouldn't have fooled around in the leaves when you should have been watching the stand with me."

"What was I supposed to watch—the flies buzzin' over our heads?" Mark asked with a frown.

Mattie rolled her eyes. "'Course not. I just think you should have been sitting here by me and not foolin' around. Guess the game with the glicker wasn't so much fun after all, huh?"

Choosing to ignore his sister's last remark, Mark took a seat on the stool and folded his arms. "All right, I'll just sit here and be *extraordinarily* bored."

"Extraordi-what?"

"Extraordinarily. It means *very* or *unusually*," Mark said.

"Why didn't you just say you're very bored instead of using a big word I don't understand?"

"I like big words. They're fun to use."

"Not for me," Mattie said with a shake of her head.

Mark closed his eyes and let the sun beat down on his face. It might be fall, but today it felt almost like summer.

Meow! Meow!

Mark opened his eyes and looked down. His fluffy gray cat, Lucky, sat on the ground by his stool, staring up at him.

"Kumme," Mark said, patting the side of his leg.

Lucky didn't have to be asked twice. She leaped into Mark's lap and started licking his hand with her sandpapery tongue.

Mark smiled and stroked the top of Lucky's head.

"You're such a nice *katz*."

"It's a good thing your cat wasn't here when that big dog came around," Mattie said. "Most dogs don't like cats, you know."

"That's true," Mark agreed. "But Lucky can run really fast, and she'd have probably climbed up a tree, like she does when your dog, Twinkles, chases her."

Mattie looked like she was going to say something more when their thirteen-year-old brother, Russell, showed up.

"What happened to my pile of leaves?" Russell asked, frowning. "I worked really hard raking them yesterday."

Mark explained about the big dog that had made a mess of the leaves.

"Couldn't you have done anything to stop him?" Russell asked, pushing a hunk of his blond hair away from his blue eyes.

"I tried, but the exuberant hund wouldn't listen."

"The what?" Mattie asked, looking at Mark.

"Exuberant. It means *lively* or *frisky*."

"That's a fact," Mattie said. "The frisky, exuberant dog had a mind of its own. He ate the whole tray of Mom's kichlin, too. I'll bet it was a stray and has no home."

Russell placed his hand on Mark's shoulder. "It doesn't look like you're that busy here, so how about helping me rake up the leaves? After that, we'll put them in the wheelbarrow and haul 'em around back to the compost pile. Guess I should have put 'em there in the first place."

"I'd rather not rake leaves," Mark said. "Besides, Mattie needs my help with the stand."

"You weren't worried about that when you were

foolin' around with your glicker," Mattie said. "I'm sure I can manage on my own for a while—especially since we haven't been that busy anyway."

Mark knew Mattie was right, but he didn't think it was fair that she got to sit and read a book while he helped Russell rake leaves. Well, then again, maybe he would find his marble while they were raking up the leaves. At least that would make it worth all the trouble he'd had here today.

CHAPTER 2

Sticky Pickles

That evening during supper, Mattie glanced over at Mark and noticed his frown. He'd been unhappy ever since he lost his marble this afternoon. She couldn't blame him for being upset, but if he'd stayed at the produce stand with her instead of tossing the marble into the leaves, he'd have it with him right now. So in some ways, it kind of served him right.

"How'd things go at the stand today?" Dad asked, passing a bowl of mashed potatoes to Mattie.

"Not so well," she said. "We only sold a few things, and that wasn't till this afternoon, after Mom brought us our lunch."

"That's too bad," Dad said. "I stopped by my brother Aaron's house this afternoon, and he said Harold and Mary sold all the pumpkins you'd given them, as well as most of their other produce."

Mattie frowned. "I'll bet we would have done better if we hadn't given them half our pumpkins."

Mark gave a nod. "The first lady who came by our stand probably would've bought a pumpkin from us if we'd had some bigger ones to choose from. But no—all the big pumpkins went to Harold and Mary."

"Where's your spirit of generosity?" Mom asked. "Don't you realize how good it feels when we give to others?"

"I suppose it does," Mattie said. "But since Mark and I didn't sell any of our pumpkins, we didn't make one bit of money for ourselves today. Though we did send two different customers over to our cousins' stand, since we didn't have what they wanted."

"It was really nice of you to do that, but don't worry, you'll have other chances to earn money," Dad said.

"That's correct," Russell put in. "Grandpa Miller's always lookin' for someone to help him with chores."

Their eleven-year-old brother, Calvin, bobbed his blond head. "I helped Grandpa clean out his barn a few weeks ago, and he gave me some money when we were done."

"It's nice to earn money," Dad said, handing the platter of ham to Mark. "But we should be willing to help others even without getting paid. The Bible tells us in Philippians 2:4 that we shouldn't look to our own interests, but to the interests of others."

"Our *daed*'s right," sixteen-year-old Ike agreed, pushing a strand of red hair out of his blue eyes. "It's a real good feeling to do something nice for someone."

Mom nodded in agreement.

"I did something nice for Russell when I helped him rake the leaves that big dog scattered today," Mark said.

"Did you do it with a smile on your face?" Mom asked, reaching over to wipe some mashed potatoes from three-year-old Ada's face.

"No, he sure didn't," Russell promptly answered before Mark could reply. "He grumbled about it the whole time."

"That's 'cause I was upset about losin' the glicker Grandpa Troyer gave me."

Ike tapped Mark's shoulder. "Maybe the marble will turn up someday."

"Well, I'm gonna keep looking," Mark said.

"That's fine," Dad said. "Just don't spend time looking for the marble when you should be doing your chores."

Mark shook his head. "I won't."

"Where do you think the marble could be?" Calvin asked.

"I'm not sure," Mark replied. "I didn't find it when Russell and I raked up the leaves and unloaded 'em on the compost heap."

"If I find the glicker, can I keep it?" asked Perry, who was five and also had blond hair like Dad's.

"No!" Mark said quickly. "If you find the marble, you must give it back to me right away."

Perry blinked like he might be about to cry, but Mom turned his attention to something else when she put two olives on his plate.

Perry loved olives and liked to put them on the ends of his fingers before popping them into his mouth. Little sister Ada didn't care for olives, but she liked pickles very much. Mark liked pickles, too, but Mattie preferred olives—especially the green ones stuffed with pimento.

✿

Mark noticed that there was only one pickle left, and he was about to reach for it when Ada hollered, "*Bickel!* Bickel!"

Thinking someone might give the last pickle to Ada, Mark quickly snatched it, and—*chomp! chomp!*—it was gone!

"Bickel! Bickel! Bickel!" Ada screamed. Tears ran down her red cheeks that almost matched her hair. "I want a bickel!"

"Calm down, Ada." Mom patted Ada's back, then she turned to Mark and said, "It was greedy of you to eat that whole pickle when you could have given Ada half."

"Sorry," Mark mumbled. "But you know how much I like bickels."

"I understand, but Ada likes them, too." Mom pointed to the door leading to the basement. "Would you please go downstairs and get another jar of pickles?"

"Okay, Mom." Mark leaped out of his chair and hurried down the stairs to the basement. He was happy to get a jar of Mom's homemade pickles because it meant he could have another pickle, too.

Mark found several jars of pickles on the shelf where Mom kept her canning jars. He chose the jar that had the biggest pickles in it, and when he reached for it, a large black cricket jumped out from behind another jar.

"Wow, he's a big one!" Mark exclaimed. "Boy would I love to catch this one!" Mark had caught crickets before and kept them in a small aquarium, just long enough to observe them for a while before releasing the insects back outside. Mark loved watching the bugs eat when he gave them small pieces of lettuce.

Thinking better of the idea of trying to catch this cricket, he looked at the insect and then at the jar of pickles in his hand. *Guess I'd better not deal with the bug right now*, he decided. *Mom will either come lookin' for me or send someone else down to see what's takin' so long.*

Running up the stairs, Mark hurried back to the kitchen. "Want me to open it?" he asked Mom after he'd set the jar on the table.

She nodded. "And when you do, the first pickle goes to Ada. Understand?"

"Jah." Mark grabbed the lid of the jar and gave it a twist. It didn't open.

"Want me to do that for you?" Ike asked.

"I'm sure I can get it." Mark twisted a little harder this time, but the lid still wouldn't budge.

"Why don't you take it over to the sink and run some warm water over the lid?" Mom suggested.

Mark did as she suggested, and then he carried the jar back to the table. Gripping the lid tightly and gritting his teeth, he cranked on the lid with all his strength. *Swoosh!* The lid came right off. Mark was about to reach inside the jar for a pickle when Ada bumped his arm and hollered, "Bickel!" The jar slipped out of Mark's hands and toppled over.

Mark took a step backward, but not quick enough. The pickles spilled onto the floor, splattering sticky juice all over, including his shoes. Some even splashed him in the face.

Mom gasped. Mattie plugged her nose and said, "Phew! That pickle juice sure does stink!" Dad's eyebrows lifted high on his forehead. Mark's brothers chuckled. Ada started to howl.

Mark moaned. This had not been a very good day. He and Mattie hadn't made any money at the stand this morning. He'd lost his marble in the pile of leaves. Then he'd helped Russell rake the leaves back into a pile. There was a big cricket in the basement, and he'd missed the chance to catch it. Now he had a smelly, sticky pickle mess to clean up.

The pickles were slippery, and whenever Mark tried to pick one up, it slipped through his fingers and fell back to the floor. "This isn't working," he said with a groan.

"Here, let me do that." Mom squatted down beside him. She looked over at Mark and slowly shook her head. "You smell like pickle juice, so you'd better let me take over here while you go wash up."

"Danki, Mom," Mark said before scurrying down the hall toward the bathroom.

❖

That night when it was time for bed, Mattie hurried to the bathroom to wash her face and brush her teeth. She figured if she got there before anyone else she wouldn't have to stand out in the hall and wait.

First Mattie washed her face with a warm washcloth. Then she removed the pins from the bun she wore at the back of her head. As she brushed her long red hair, she counted. . .one. . .two. . .three. . .four. . .five. . . She'd just reached the number twenty when someone pounded on the door.

"Hurry up, Mattie! You're taking too long," Mark hollered from the other side of the door.

"Go away! I'm busy brushing my hair!"

Bang! Bang! Bang! "Come on, Mattie! I need in there now!"

Mattie kept counting and brushing her hair. She didn't stop until she got to one hundred. Grandma Miller had told Mattie once that she brushed her hair one hundred times every night. Mattie figured it would be a good idea if she did the same.

Bang! Bang! "Mattie, are you ever coming out?"

"I'm not done yet. I need to brush my teeth." Mattie put toothpaste on her toothbrush, opened her mouth real wide, and took her time brushing every one of her teeth. When she was done, she rinsed out her mouth with cold water. When she opened the bathroom door, Mark was standing in the hall with a scowl on his face.

"It's about time," he grumbled. "You were selfish hoggin' the bathroom like that."

"I wouldn't talk about being selfish if I were you," Mattie said with her hands on her hips. "You've been doing selfish things all day."

"Have not."

"Have so."

"Have—"

"Mattie!" Mom called from the kitchen. "Would you tuck Ada and Perry into bed while I finish cleaning up in here? There's still some of that sticky pickle juice on the floor that I missed before."

Mattie wished she didn't have to tuck her little brother and sister into bed. "Why don't you take care of Perry while I see to Ada?" Mattie asked Mark.

He shook his head. "Mom asked you to do it, not me."

"I know, but I want to read awhile before I go to bed," Mattie said. "If I have to tuck both Ada and Perry in, it'll take too long."

"It won't take you any longer to tuck them in than it did to comb your hair and brush your teeth while I waited out here in the hall." Mark opened the bathroom door and quickly stepped inside.

"I wish I were Mom and Dad's only child," Mattie mumbled as she tromped up the stairs.

CHAPTER 3

A Day with Grandpa and Grandma

The following Saturday, Mark and Mattie were invited to spend the day with Grandma and Grandpa Miller. Mark hoped he and Grandpa would do something fun together— maybe go fishing or take a walk in the woods. However, he was disappointed when Grandpa announced that he and Grandma would be taking the twins to some yard sales today. Mark thought going to a yard sale would be boring, but at least it was a better way to spend a Saturday than selling produce at their roadside stand and not making any money.

As they traveled down the road in Grandpa and Grandma's buggy, Mark's eyes grew heavy. He'd stayed up later than usual last night, first in the basement looking for the cricket, which he'd had no luck in finding. He had spent more than an hour in the basement, looking in every nook and cranny, behind all the jars on the canning shelf, and even in Mom's washing machine. Mark thought it would be awesome if he'd caught the big insect and kept it in his room overnight, listening to it chirp. The last time he'd done that, with the ones he'd caught and put in the aquarium, it was a full-blown chorus as each cricket seemed to try and outdo the other with its musical song.

Then, when Mark had finally given up on the cricket, he'd gone back to his room, searching for big words in the dictionary. He'd found two new ones that he liked really well. They were *extravagant* and *conscientious*. Now he just needed to wait for the right time to say one or both of these big words.

Feeling the buggy's rocking movement and hearing the steady *clippety-clop* of the horse's hooves made Mark even sleepier. His head lulled against the seat, and he closed his eyes. Pretty soon he was fast asleep. He'd only been sleeping a few minutes, however, when Mattie bumped his arm.

Mark's eyes snapped open. "What do you want, Mattie? Couldn't you see that I was sleeping?"

"Sorry for waking ya, but I was wonderin' if I could borrow your catcher's mitt when we get home. Thought I might ask Calvin or Russell to throw the baseball to me so I can get better at catching."

Mark shook his head. "My friend John Schrock gave me that catcher's mitt for my birthday, so I don't think it'd be right if I loaned it out."

"I doubt that John would care."

Mark said nothing—just closed his eyes again and tried to sleep.

Mattie tapped his arm. "I have another question."

"What's that?"

"Did you feed Twinkles this morning?"

"Now why would I wanna do that?" Mark asked.

"Twinkles is your hund, not mine."

"I know, but when you went outside to give Lucky her breakfast, I asked if you'd feed Twinkles, too." Mattie nudged his arm again. "Remember, Mark?"

" 'Course I remember."

"So did you feed her or not?"

He shook his head.

"How come?"

" 'Cause it's your responsibility to take care of your hund, and you oughta be conscientious enough to do it."

Mattie's forehead wrinkled. "Consci—what?"

"The word is *conscientious*. It means *reliable*."

"I am reliable, but I thought you could feed Twinkles as a favor to me."

"I have enough of my own chores to do," Mark said.

Mattie folded her arms and frowned. "The only reason I asked you to feed Twinkles is because I was busy helping Mom do the breakfast dishes. I didn't think I'd have time to get Twinkles fed before Grandma and Grandpa picked us up."

"We would have waited for you to feed the dog," Grandma called over her shoulder.

"See," Mark said. "You should have told Grandma and Grandpa that Twinkles needed to be fed." He was glad Grandma had heard what Mattie said.

"But I didn't, and you didn't feed her, so now the poor hund is probably starving to death. You could have at least told me you didn't feed her," Mattie persisted.

"She won't starve from missing one meal." Grandpa glanced back at Mattie. "Just remember to feed her as soon as you get home. Oh, and Mark, it would have been nice if you'd fed Twinkles for your sister."

Mattie looked over at Mark and said, "Don't worry—I'll never ask you to feed my hund again, and don't ask me to feed your katz either."

❖

By the time they had stopped at three yard sales, Mattie was bored. She hadn't seen anything that interested her at all. There were a lot of baby clothes, some farm equipment, furniture, dishes, and some canning jars, which Grandma bought, but nothing Mattie wanted. Grandpa had found a new handle for the one that broke on his rake, and he'd also purchased a metal milk can to store birdseed in for the winter on their back porch.

This third yard sale had something different from the first two they had gone to, however. There was a small concession stand set up selling hot dogs, barbeque sandwiches, homemade cookies, and peanut butter fudge. They also had bottled water available for anyone who was thirsty.

"How would you like something to eat?" Grandpa asked the twins. "Your grandma and I are getting a little hungry from all this yard-sale hopping, and I see there's some food tables set up over there under those big maple trees."

"I'm hungry, too," Mark answered.

"Same here," Mattie agreed.

They all decided to get hot dogs, except for Grandpa. He chose the pork barbeque sandwich. Grandma reminded everyone that she'd made peanut butter cookies yesterday, and they'd have those once they got back to their house.

"I'll have just ketchup on my hot dog," Mattie told the

teenage boy making the sandwiches.

"I'd like mustard and relish on mine," Mark said when it was his turn to choose.

Grandma smiled when the boy asked her what she would like on her hot dog. "Ketchup, mustard, relish, and onions, please. I want the works."

There were chairs and a few tables set up, also under the shade of the trees, and they all took a seat to eat their lunch. Mark and Mattie were in a conversation about what they hoped to find at the next place they were going to. As Grandpa and Grandma Miller ate, they watched the small crowd of people looking over the items for sale.

"I hope I can find a yo-yo," Mark said to Mattie as he wiped a glob of mustard off the side of his mouth.

"I'm not sure if I'm looking for anything in particular." Mattie took another bite of her hot dog. "I thought you wanted a *new* yo-yo and not another used one."

"If I find one that's better than the one I have, that would be okay with me. I just have to—"

Mattie looked at Mark, wondering why he'd stopped in midsentence. Her gaze followed the direction her brother was looking, and Mattie's heart almost stopped beating. It felt like it had jumped into her throat.

"Carolyn! Carolyn! Are you all right?" Grandpa looked at Grandma with a panicked expression.

Mattie watched in horror as Grandma pointed first to her throat and then to her mouth. It looked like she was trying to tell Grandpa something, but all she could do was make little gasping noises.

Grandpa gave Grandma's back a couple of thumps, but it didn't seem to help. "Can someone please help us?"

Grandpa shouted. "My wife seems to be choking!"

It was like someone sounded an alarm, and several people came running over. They must have heard the urgency in Grandpa's voice.

"Grandma's turning blue," Mark whimpered, reaching out to hold Mattie's hand.

Mattie was really scared. She'd never seen anyone choke like this before, except little Ada, but she had only sputtered on milk while she was drinking it. This was different, though. Grandma couldn't talk, and it looked like she was having trouble breathing.

Mattie quickly said a silent prayer, *Lord, please help my grandma.*

"She needs to stand up!" the teenage boy who'd given them the hot dogs yelled as he raced over and got behind Grandma.

Mattie's fear increased as Grandpa helped Grandma stand. What was this boy going to do to their grandma?

Mattie watched helplessly as the boy wrapped his arms around Grandma's waist from behind, made a fist with both hands together, and made quick upward thrusts into the upper part of her stomach. He did this only a few times, and all of a sudden a big piece of hot dog flew out of Grandma's mouth. Almost immediately Grandma coughed and was able to breathe again.

Mattie breathed a sigh of relief as Grandma, her face turning red, whispered, "Guess I should learn to take smaller bites."

It seemed like everyone, strangers included, went "*whew*" at the same time as Mark and Mattie.

Grandpa smiled and shook the boy's hand, thanking

him for saving Grandma's life. "What is your name, son?"

"Well, my real name is Anthony, but most folks just call me Tony," he answered, looking a little embarrassed at all the attention he was getting. "Guess it's a good thing I was listening in class the day they taught us first aid."

"What was it that you did to my grandma?" Mattie asked.

"That's called the Heimlich maneuver," Tony answered. "When someone is choking and can't breathe, that's what you do to dislodge the food or obstruction in their windpipe. There's even a way to do the procedure on yourself, if you happen to be alone and start choking."

"Well, I'm glad you were here to help. Thank you so much." Grandma patted Tony's arm. "Now I want everyone to quit worrying about me. I'm fine now, and you know what? I'm still hungry, not to mention eager to see some of the other yard sales that await us today."

After the frightening experience was over, it felt good to relax, knowing Grandma was going to be all right.

"I know one thing," Mark said to Mattie after they'd finished their lunch. "I'm gonna read up on this Heimlich maneuver. I think everyone should know how to do that."

❁

At the next yard sale they went to, Mattie spotted a table full of toys and games. She was on her way to look at them when she noticed a pretty snow globe on one of the tables. Inside the globe was a garden scene with flowers, a butterfly, and even a frog. Mark must have seen the globe, too, because he reached for it at the same time as Mattie.

"You'd better not touch it," Mattie said. "It looks

breakable. Besides, I saw it first."

"Don't be so selfish, Mattie. I have just as much right to look at the snow globe as you do." Mark snatched up the globe and gave it a shake. Colored pieces of fake snow swirled all around inside the miniature world. It was beautiful!

"It's my turn now," Mattie said, taking the globe out of Mark's hands. It was the prettiest snow globe she'd ever seen. It was not only a globe but also a music box, so that made it even more special.

Mattie had only been holding the globe a few seconds and was getting ready to wind it up so she could listen to the song it played, when Mark snatched it right back. "I wanna see that!"

"Hey! I wasn't done looking at it yet. I wanna hear what song it plays." Mattie grabbed hold of the snow globe, but Mark wouldn't let go. Mattie gritted her teeth and tugged. Mark did the same. Suddenly, Mattie let go, but so did Mark. *Crash!*—the snow globe hit the ground and broke into several pieces. It was ruined!

Mattie gasped. Mark moaned. Grandma and Grandpa came running over with worried expressions.

"What happened?" Grandma asked.

Mattie quickly explained. Mark just stood, staring at the ground.

"If Mattie had let me hold the snow globe, it wouldn't have fallen and broken into pieces," Mark said.

Mattie frowned. "If you had let *me* hold the globe, it wouldn't have broken."

Deep wrinkles formed across Grandpa's forehead. "Just a minute here. It sounds to me like you were both in the wrong, and now you'll have to pay for the broken globe."

Tears welled in Mattie's eyes. "But I only have fifty cents, and the globe is two dollars."

"I have fifty cents, too," Mark said. "So between me and Mattie, we just have one dollar."

"You two can pay for half, and I'll pay the rest of it," Grandpa said. "But you will both have to do a few chores for me and Grandma today to work off your debt."

Mattie looked down, disappointed that they'd be leaving the yard sale empty-handed. Mark's frown let her know that he was unhappy about that, too.

"As soon as you pay for the snow globe, I think we should go home," Grandma told Grandpa. "I've had enough yard sales for one day."

Grandpa gave a nod. "Mark, you can start by helping me tie the milk can I bought at the last yard sale onto the back of the buggy. It's really too crowded for it to ride inside the buggy." Then he looked at both of the twins and said, "If you two don't get over your selfish attitudes, you're going to have a bumpy ride ahead."

"What do you mean?" Mark asked.

"If you keep being selfish, you'll have lots of problems, just like you would if you were riding on a very bumpy road and got jostled around," Grandpa explained.

Mattie couldn't imagine having any more problems than she did right now, and she sure hoped they wouldn't have a bumpy ride home.

CHAPTER 4

Tent for Two

"I'm glad we don't have to go to any yard sales today," Mark told Mattie as they entered the barn the following Saturday morning.

"I know," Mattie agreed. "After what happened last week with Grandma choking and then the snow globe breaking, I don't care if I ever go to another yard sale again—or eat a hot dog either."

When the twins had gone back to Grandpa and Grandma's house after leaving the yard sale, Mattie had helped Grandma with some things in the house, and Mark helped Grandpa do some cleaning in the barn. After Mark and Mattie had eaten some cookies before going home for the day, Grandma had said she hoped they'd learned a good lesson about the consequences of selfishness.

"Let's climb into the hayloft," Mark said, distracting Mattie from her thoughts. "Then we can swing on the rope that hangs up there."

Mattie shook her head. "I don't want to do that. It'll make my stomach do little flip-flops."

"Okay then, let's find Lucky and play with her. I'll get some catnip, and we can tease her with it."

"It's not nice to tease," Mattie said. "Besides, I'd rather play with my hund than your katz."

Mark shrugged. "Do whatever you like. I'm goin' up the ladder to the hayloft." He hurried away and was almost to the ladder when Dad entered the barn.

"Your *mamm* and I are going to town to do some shopping," he said. "So we need you two to go into the house and keep an eye on your little sister and brother. They're napping right now, and when they wake up, you'll need to keep them entertained until we get home."

"Why can't one of our older brothers keep an eye on Ada and Perry?" Mark asked.

"Because Ike and Russell are visiting some of their friends, and Calvin went fishing with Grandpa today."

Mark thumped the side of his head. "Oh, that's right; I forgot about that. Wish now I'd gone fishin' with them."

Mattie didn't want to keep an eye on her little brother and sister, but she knew if Mom and Dad were leaving, she and Mark didn't have much choice. So she tapped Mark on the shoulder and said, "Come on, let's go inside."

As Mom and Dad's horse and buggy pulled out of the yard, Mark followed Mattie into the house, shuffling his feet and grumbling, "It's not fair. I really wanted some time to play."

"Maybe we can find something fun to do in the house," Mattie said.

"Sure hope so," he said.

Once they were inside, Mattie suggested they go to the kitchen and have some of Mom's peanut butter cookies and a glass of milk.

"That's a really *gut* idea." Mark smacked his lips. "Just

thinking about Mom's tasty kichlin makes me hungerich."

Mattie climbed onto a stool, took the cookie jar off the counter, and set it on the table. Then, while she got out two glasses, Mark went to the refrigerator for the milk.

The twins took seats at the table, and Mark poured milk into their glasses while Mattie gave them each two cookies.

Mark reached for a cookie, bumped his glass, and—*clunk!*—knocked it over. "Oh no," he groaned, quickly grabbing for some napkins to wipe up the mess before it soaked the cookies.

"You should have been more careful and watched what you were doing," Mattie said.

Mark frowned. "You don't have to act so bossy." He picked up the container of milk and poured himself another glass. *Slurp! Slurp!* He drank it all down and poured some more. When he dunked his cookie into the milk, it fell to the bottom of the glass. "Oh great! Now my kichlin's stuck, and it's gonna get all mushy."

"Why don't you get a spoon and see if you can get it out that way?" Mattie suggested.

"I was just gonna do that." Mark got out a spoon and put it in the glass, but the cookie remained stuck. He turned the glass upside down and tapped on the bottom while tipping the glass up to his mouth. *Whoosh!*—the cookie fell out, and the broken, soggy pieces stuck to his face.

Mattie giggled. Mark grunted and reached for a napkin to wipe his face. "I'm done with the cookies! I'm going back outside."

"You can't do that," Mattie said. "Dad told us we have to stay in the house to keep an eye on Perry and Ada."

"But they're taking a nap. If we go outside on the porch, we can hear them if they wake up."

"Maybe you're right," Mattie agreed. "I'll put the cookie jar back on the counter, and then we can go."

"I'm goin' now. I'll see ya out there!" Mark hurried out the back door, letting the screen door slam.

❀

Mark had been sitting on the porch step, playing with his old yo-yo for about ten minutes, when Mattie joined him. "Are Ada and Perry still sleeping?" he asked.

"They must be," Mattie said, "because I didn't hear a peep out of them while I was putting the cookies away. Good thing, too. The way you let that screen door slam, it's a wonder they didn't wake up."

"Oops, sorry. Guess I wasn't thinkin' about that. Anyways, it's good that they didn't wake up. Now, why don't we play a game of hide-and-seek?" Mark suggested.

"There's no place to hide here on the porch," Mattie said.

"We can play in the yard. There are lots of places to hide out there."

Mattie shook her head. "We can't go into the yard. We wouldn't be able to hear Ada and Perry from there."

"I'm sure I can. I've got good ears."

"Oh, alright," Mattie finally agreed. "But we'd better not go too far from the house."

Mark stepped off the porch and raced into the yard. Mattie was close behind him.

"Tag! You're it!" Mark shouted, tapping Mattie's shoulder.

"I thought we were going to play hide-and-seek," Mattie said.

Mark shook his head. "I changed my mind. I'd rather play tag instead."

Mattie folded her arms. "I don't want to play tag. I'd rather play hide-and-seek."

"It was my idea to play a game, so I should be the one to choose."

"Okay," Mattie said with a huff. "You'd better run fast because here I come, and you know I can run really fast!"

Mark took off across the yard. He knew Mattie could run faster than him, so he darted behind the house and ducked behind a bush. A few seconds later, he heard Mattie calling, "Mark, where are you?"

Mark held very still and didn't say a word.

"You'd better not be hiding from me. We're supposed to be playing tag, not hide-and-seek!"

Mark put his hand over his mouth so Mattie wouldn't hear him snickering. He thought it was fun to play a trick on her.

"Mark Miller, if you're hiding, you'd better come out and show yourself right now!"

It sounded like Mattie's voice was getting closer and closer, so Mark crouched down a little lower behind the bush. He waited until Mattie had gone a little past him, then he leaped out and hollered, "Tag! You're it!"

She shook her finger at him and frowned. "It was my turn to tag you, not the other way around. And you shouldn't be sneakin' up on me like that!"

"Sorry, I just wanted to have a little fun. You can run now, and I'll chase you."

Mattie shook her head. "I'm done playing this silly game. Besides, we really should be in the house so we can hear when Ada and Perry wake up."

"Oh, all right." Mark took off across the yard like a racehorse, leaped onto the porch, and hurried into the house. Mattie never knew her brother could run that fast. He must have been practicing when she wasn't around.

Mattie remembered the last time Mark had played ball at school. He hadn't been able to run fast at all, and when he'd fallen, some of the kids made fun of him. If they'd seen him sprint across the lawn just now, they sure wouldn't be laughing.

"Now what should we do?" Mattie asked when she entered the house and found Mark sitting on the sofa in the living room, trying to fix the yo-yo that had gotten all tangled in his pocket.

"I know—let's make a tent!" Mark said excitedly. "We can drape a blanket over some folding chairs and anchor it with some of Mom's clothespins."

"That's a real good idea," Mattie said. "We can pretend we're on a camping trip."

Mark bobbed his head. "It'll be fun. We can fix ourselves a snack to take in there, too."

Mattie's eyebrows rose. "Are you hungry again? We just had some kichlin and milk awhile ago."

Mark grinned. "I'm always hungerich."

"Okay, we'll have a snack." Mattie smiled. "Oh, and I have another idea about the tent."

"What's that?"

"We can put a blanket and some pillows inside and pretend they're sleeping bags."

"Great! I'll get the blanket and clothespins to make the tent while you fix us a snack," Mark said.

Mattie frowned. "You don't have to be so bossy. Maybe I want to get the blanket and clothespins. Did you ever think about that?"

"I wasn't tryin' to be bossy. I just know that I'm better at makin' a tent than you are, and you're good at fixin' snacks."

"I guess you're right," Mattie agreed. "Okay, I'll fix us something to eat while you build the tent."

"I'll put the tent together here in the living room. See you inside the tent soon, Mattie!" Mark hurried out of the room, leaving Mattie to head for the kitchen to fix their snacks.

❧

Mattie took some cheese slices from the refrigerator and got out a box of crackers. Then she grabbed two apples from the bowl of fruit on the table, placed everything on a tray, and took it to the living room. Mark was already there and had draped a big blanket over the back of four chairs.

"I just need to clip the edges of this blanket with a few clothespins, and we'll be all set," he announced.

Mattie smiled. "I'll put our snacks on the little table by the sofa, and then I can help you clip the blanket in place."

Mark shook his head. "I can do it myself. Why don't you get the pillows off the sofa and put them inside the tent?"

Mattie thought Mark was being bossy again, but she was eager to get into the tent, so she did what he asked. By the time she'd taken the pillows off the sofa, Mark had the blanket pinned in place.

"I'll go in first," he said. "Then you can hand the tray of snacks in to me before you come inside."

Mattie didn't think it was fair that Mark got to go in the tent first, but again, she said nothing and did what he asked.

Once Mattie handed the snacks to Mark and had crawled into the tent herself, she relaxed against the pillows. Then she closed her eyes and tried to imagine that they were in a real tent, camping in the woods.

"Wake up, sleepyhead," Mark said, tickling Mattie under the chin.

She opened her eyes and pushed his hand away. "I'm not sleeping. I was pretending we were camping in a real tent."

Mark smiled. "Sure hope Dad takes us camping next summer, like he promised he'd do."

"I'm sure he will, but next summer's a long ways off, so we may as well enjoy our little tent right here in the house where it's warm and cozy. There aren't any *keffer* to worry about in here either."

"That's true. No bugs and no snakes."

Mattie nodded. She didn't like most bugs, but she knew Mark was really afraid of snakes. Even so, he still enjoyed camping, and in all the times they'd gone with Dad, they'd only seen a couple of snakes, and they weren't the poisonous kind.

"Why don't we eat our snack now?" Mattie suggested.

"That's a good idea." Mark grabbed an apple and took a big bite. "Yum! This is appeditlich!"

"The cheese and crackers are delicious, too," Mattie

said after she'd eaten one of each.

Mark gave a nod. "Jah, and since Perry and Ada are still asleep we don't have to share our snacks with them."

"Or the tent, either," Mattie said. "I'll bet when Ada and Perry see the tent they'll want to come in."

"Well, they're not going to," Mark announced with a determined expression. "This tent isn't big enough for the four of us. It's a tent for two!"

When Mark and Mattie finished their snacks, they closed their eyes and rested on the pillows. Mattie was almost asleep when she heard Ada and Perry chattering away as they tromped down the stairs.

"Oh no," Mark groaned. "Let's be real quiet. Maybe they won't know we're here."

A few minutes later Perry stuck his head into the tent. "Whatcha doin'?" he asked.

"We made a tent, and you can't come in 'cause there isn't enough room," Mark said, rolling over onto his side.

Perry scowled at him. *"Eegesinnisch."*

"I'm not selfish," Mark said. "There just isn't room for you to come in. Besides, I'm the one who made the tent."

Just then Ada poked her head in. She held out her arms to Mattie and whimpered.

"We'll either have to let her come in or leave the tent," Mattie said, looking at Mark.

"Then you'd better go out, because if we let Ada in, Perry will think he can come in, too."

"Then why don't you go out with Ada and Perry and let me stay in the tent?"

Mark shook his head. "I made the tent, and I'm not leaving!"

"Perry's right. You are eegesinnisch!" Mattie grabbed the empty tray and crawled out of the tent. She would fix Ada and Perry a snack and take them outside to play. Mark could have his silly old tent for two all to himself!

❧

Mark lay there, staring at the blanket above him and thinking about the camping trip they'd taken after school let out last year and how much fun it had been. He especially enjoyed the meals Mom had cooked over the campfire. It had also been fun to listen to the stories Dad had shared about his childhood as they all sat around the campfire every night before going to bed.

Mark tried once more to untangle his yo-yo, and after undoing several knots that had formed, he finally got the string smoothed out. *Sure wish I could have bought a new yo-yo by now*, he thought. *I'd even settle for a used one if it was nicer than this one.*

Mark's eyes grew heavy, and he was almost asleep when he heard a loud—*cr-a-a-sh!* It sounded like it had come from the kitchen. He crawled out of the tent and raced into the kitchen, where he found Mattie, Ada, and Perry in the middle of the room, staring at the cookie jar, which was broken.

"What happened?" he asked, looking at Mattie.

"When I wasn't watching, Perry climbed onto a stool to get the cookie jar, and he knocked it off the counter. As you can see, the jar's broken, and there are smashed cookies all over the floor!"

"That's too bad. I think you'd better clean up the mess while I take Ada and Perry outside to play," Mark said.

Mattie frowned. "That's not fair. Why should I have to clean up the mess?"

"I'll bet if Mom were here she'd make Ada and Perry clean up their own mess."

"I don't think so," Mattie said. "They're not good at cleaning things up, and they'd probably make an even bigger mess. Besides, they might get cut picking up the broken pieces of the cookie jar."

"Maybe we should wait till Mom and Dad get home, and then Mom can clean up the mess."

Mattie shook her head. "We were supposed to be in the house keeping an eye on Ada and Perry. Mom's not gonna be happy when she finds out that her jar got broken, and I need to clean up the mess and throw away the cookies that are on the floor before she gets here."

"Fine then—you clean this up, and I'll watch Ada and Perry." Mark quickly herded his little brother and sister out the back door, leaving Mattie to clean up the kitchen.

CHAPTER 5

Zoo-rific!

"Guess what?" Mark asked Mattie as they rode their bicycle built for two home from school on the first Monday of October.

"What?" Mattie questioned, leaning forward so she was closer to Mark's ear.

"During recess this afternoon I was talking to my friend Dan Yoder. He said his folks are taking him and his sister, Becky, to see the animals at the Farm at Walnut Creek this Saturday. It'll be just like goin' to a petting zoo, only I bet it'll be even better." He grinned. "It's gonna be a zoo-rific day!"

"How nice. I'm sure they'll have a lot of fun." Mattie sighed. "I've always wanted to go there, but I guess that's never gonna happen."

Mark grinned. "Jah, it is, Mattie. Dan invited me to go with 'em, and he said you could come, too."

"Really?"

"That's right," Mark said with a nod. "I can't wait till we get home so we can tell Mom about this and ask if we can go."

Mattie had never been to an actual petting zoo before,

except she did get to pet some of the animals at the Geauga County Fair when they'd gone to Burton to visit Grandpa and Grandma Troyer two years ago.

"Let's pedal as hard as we can so we can get home quickly and talk to Mom," Mattie hollered in Mark's ear. She was really excited about this and hoped they could go.

"That's fine with me!" Mark shouted as he pumped his legs harder and steered the bike in the direction of home. "Dan even said we'll get to ride in a horse-drawn wagon to see most of the animals, so we'll get a good look at 'em, up close and personal."

When the twins pedaled the bike into their yard a short time later, they parked it near the barn and hurried across the yard, where Mom was taking clothes off the line.

"You got home quickly today," Mom said. "I was planning to fix you a snack and thought I had time to take the clothes down, but here you are." Mom clucked her tongue. "Your older brothers aren't even home from school yet."

"We pedaled hard so we could get here quickly," Mark said breathlessly. "Mattie and I have a question we want to ask you."

Mom tipped her head. "Oh, what's that?"

"Mark's friend Dan invited us to go with him and his family to the Farm at Walnut Creek this Saturday." Mattie jumped up and down. "Can we go, Mom? Can we, please?"

"You'll have to check with your daed first," Mom said. "But I'm pretty sure it'll be alright."

Mark grabbed Mattie's hand and whirled her around. "Yippee! I can hardly wait to see all the animals—especially the giraffes we've heard so much about."

"You two had better calm down," Mom said. You'll make yourself *daremlich* twirling around like that."

"I'm not dizzy," Mattie said.

"You will be if you keep spinning around like that. And since your daed hasn't given his permission for you to go yet, you shouldn't get so excited."

"But you said you were pretty sure it would be alright," Mark reminded their mother.

Mom gave a nod. "But I don't want you to be disappointed if he says no."

Mark frowned. Mattie's bottom lip jutted out. "We really want to go," they said at the same time.

Mom placed one hand on the top of the twins' heads. "Your daed's in the house, so why don't you run inside and ask him right now?"

Mark grabbed Mattie's hand, and they took off for the house. They found Dad in the living room, slouched in his favorite chair. His eyes were closed, and soft snores came out of his mouth.

Mattie looked at Mark and whispered, "Do you think we should wake him?"

Mark shook his head. "We'd better not. He might get upset."

Mattie sighed. At this rate they'd *never* know if they could go with Mark's friend or not.

"Since we can't ask Dad anything right now, I'm goin' upstairs to change my clothes," Mark said. "After that, I think I'll go outside to play with Lucky awhile."

Mattie shrugged. "You can do whatever you want, but I'm staying right here till Dad wakes up." She took a seat on the sofa and folded her arms.

Mark rolled his eyes, like he often did when he thought she was being silly. "Suit yourself, but you might be in for a long wait." He hurried from the room and tromped up the stairs.

For the next several minutes Mattie continued to sit and stare at Dad, watching his chest rise and fall with steady, even breaths. She was about to give up and go to her room when Dad's eyes popped open.

"*Ach*, Mattie! How long have you been sitting there?" he asked.

"Just a little while. I was waiting for you to wake up," Mattie said. "I need to ask you an important question."

Dad opened his mouth and yawned noisily, rubbing his eyes. "What's that?"

"Mark and I have been invited to go to the Farm at Walnut Creek with his friend Dan and his family this Saturday. Mom said it was okay, but that we'd have to check with you first."

Dad yawned again and pulled his fingers through the ends of his full beard.

Mattie's heart pounded as she waited for his answer.

Dad leaned forward and smiled at Mattie. "Now don't look so worried. You have my permission to go."

Mattie was so excited, she leaped off the sofa and ran across the room. "Danki," she said, giving Dad a big hug.

❁

On Thursday morning, Mattie woke up with a sore throat. She felt achy and warm all over, too. "Oh no, this isn't good," she moaned, rolling slowly out of bed. "I can't be sick. I *won't* be sick."

Mattie winced when she swallowed. Oh, it really did hurt! She forced herself to get dressed. Then she plodded down the stairs, went to the bathroom to wash her face, and made her way slowly to the kitchen.

Mom was there, cracking eggs into a bowl. She turned to look quickly at Mattie and went back to what she was doing. "I'm glad you're up. Would you please set the table while I get breakfast started?"

Mattie said nothing—just moved at a snail's pace across the room, opened the cupboard door, and removed nine plates.

"Did you sleep well last night?" Mom asked.

Mattie shrugged her shoulders. Truth was, she hadn't slept well at all.

Mom turned to look at Mattie again, and her eyebrows pulled together. "Guess I didn't look at you closely before, but I see now that your cheeks are flushed. Are you feeling alright?" she questioned.

Mattie's gaze dropped to the floor as she slowly shook her head.

"Why, I believe you're running a fever," Mom said after she'd placed her hand on Mattie's forehead.

Mattie cringed. She was afraid of that and knew if she did have a fever, it meant she was definitely sick.

"Have a seat at the table," Mom instructed. "I'm going to get the thermometer so I can take your temperature." She hurried out of the room before Mattie could offer a word of protest.

When Mom returned, she put the thermometer under Mattie's tongue. After several minutes went by, Mom removed it.

"No school for you today," Mom said, studying the thermometer. "You do have a fever."

"My throat's sore, too, and I feel kinda achy," Mattie admitted.

Mom patted Mattie's arm. "I believe you've come down with the flu, so you need to go right back to bed."

Mattie groaned. She didn't mind missing a day of school, but she didn't like being sick. "What if I'm still *grank* on Saturday?" she wailed. "Sure don't want to miss goin' to the Farm."

"If you don't get to go this time, I'm sure there'll be another time."

Tears welled in Mattie's eyes. "I've already waited a long time to go there."

Mom gave Mattie's arm another tender pat. "Let's wait until Saturday and see how you're feeling."

Mattie closed her eyes and said a silent prayer: *Please help me to feel better by Saturday, Lord.*

❀

"Sure can't wait till Dan's folks come by to pick me and Mattie up," Mark said to Mom when he bounded into the kitchen on Saturday morning.

Mom slowly shook her head. "I'm sorry, but it'll only be you going to the Farm today. Mattie's throat is still sore, so she'll be staying home to rest."

Mark's eyebrows furrowed. "That's too bad. I know she really wanted to go."

"Jah, she did, but I talked to your daed last night, and he said he'd take our whole family there next summer, sometime after school lets out."

Mark smiled. "Oh good! That means I'll get to go there twice. Then when we go next year, I'll know a little more about the Farm and be able to point out some of the things I learn today."

"That's right," Mom agreed. "But don't rub it in to Mattie. She's upset enough about not being able to go with you and Dan's family."

Mark shook his head. "I won't say a thing about it to her."

❖

Tears streamed down Mattie's face as she stood at her bedroom window and watched Mark climb into Dan's parents' buggy. It wasn't fair that he got to go to the Farm today and she had to stay home sick. She wished Mark would have stayed home and waited until they could go together.

I'll probably never get to see all those animals, she thought.

Mattie turned from the window and crawled back into bed. A few minutes later, Mom entered the room. "I brought you some breakfast," she said, placing the tray she was carrying on the small table by Mattie's bed.

"I'm not hungerich," Mattie mumbled.

"You need to eat something," Mom said. "I fixed you some scrambled eggs. They're soft and should be easy to eat, so they shouldn't hurt your throat when you swallow."

Mattie sat up and let Mom place the tray in her lap. She knew if she didn't eat, Mom would probably stay there until she did.

"I know you're sad about not getting to go with Mark today," Mom said.

Mattie nodded and swiped at the tears on her cheeks. "Mark was selfish to go without me. He could have stayed home."

Mom placed her hand on Mattie's arm. "Aren't you being a bit selfish expecting him to stay home just because you're sick and couldn't go?"

"I—I guess." Mattie sighed. "But I'll probably never get to go to the Farm at Walnut Creek."

Mom shook her head. "That's not true. Your daed's planning to take the whole family there next summer."

"Really?"

"That's what he said."

Mattie ate a bite of scrambled egg, swallowing carefully, and then she washed it down with some of the apple juice Mom had also put on the tray. "But summer's a long ways off, and right now I'm stuck here in bed. Mark's gonna have a lot of fun today, and it's just not fair!" Mattie couldn't help feeling sorry for herself. She didn't like being sick, and she didn't like staying home when her twin brother was out having fun.

"Finish your breakfast," Mom said. "When you're done, you can read a book."

"I don't feel like reading. I wanna do something fun."

"Would you like to make some homemade paper dolls?" Mom asked.

"Will you help me make 'em?"

"I need to go downstairs right now and check on Ada and Perry, but as soon as I put them down for their naps I'll come back here, and then we can cut out some paper dolls together."

Mattie smiled. Making paper dolls with Mom wouldn't

be nearly as much fun as seeing the animals at the Farm, but at least it was something to look forward to. She couldn't help but wonder, though, what fun things Mark was doing right now with his friend.

❖

"This is going to be so much fun," Mark told Dan as they climbed aboard the large wagon that would take them on the trails to see all the animals at the Farm.

Dan nodded, and his blue eyes twinkled, so Mark knew Dan was as excited about being there as he was. "The horses pullin' this wagon are just like the ones my daed uses to plow our fields," Dan said as the boys took a seat on the wooden bench along the left side of the wagon.

"Jah," Mark agreed. "My daed uses big draft horses, too."

"And look," Dan said. "These horses have bells!"

Sure enough, Mark noticed that both of the horses hitched to the wagon had bells on their harnesses.

The Amish man who drove the wagon and would be their guide turned in his seat and said, "There are a few rules everyone needs to know about before we start through the park. You must stay in the wagon at all times and remain seated whenever the wagon is moving. You can feed some of the four-legged animals by holding the food I gave you in your hand, but most of them will need to be fed by pouring some of the feed out of the buckets and onto the floor of the wagon where they can reach it. You'll need to feed the two-legged feathered animals with beaks out of the bucket. If you don't, their sharp beaks might hurt your hands. There are some areas I'll be taking us through where the animals will be walking right up to the wagon, so hang on to your bucket, because if you drop it out of the wagon, we won't be able to stop and pick it up." He smiled and gave Mark a wink. "And feel free to ask questions about any of the animals we see."

Mark gave a nod. He was pretty sure he'd have a few questions to ask.

As they rode along, the jingling bells on the horses made it sound like Christmastime. It was interesting as their driver pointed out some goats and several sheep with long, curved horns that were called Aoudad.

"These unusual sheep come from northern Algeria," the Amish man said. "They are able to run fast up steep hills and go as long as five days without fresh water."

"Wow!" Mark exclaimed. "I sure couldn't go that long without gettin' a drink of water."

"Me neither," Dan agreed.

They rode a little farther until they came upon some deer and elk. It was fun to hold the bucket of feed out or put food on the wagon floor so the animals could eat whenever the wagon stopped.

"Oh look, there's a zebra!" Mark shouted. "I've seen pictures of zebras in books but never thought I'd see one up close."

When a zebra came up to the wagon to be fed, Mark reached out and stroked the animal behind its ear. It felt soft and silky, just like Dad's buggy horse.

"What kind of a zebra is this?" Mark asked their guide.

"It's called the Grevy's zebra, and it's the largest species of zebra. It's also able to run as fast as forty miles per hour."

"Now that's really somethin'!" Mark whistled. "Sure wish I could run that fast."

Next, they saw an ostrich with a long neck and pointed beak. Mark held his bucket tightly as the ostrich eagerly stuck its beak into the bucket to get some food. In and out! In and out! The big bird's head bobbed back and forth.

"I think this enormous bird is tryin' to eat all the food," Mark said.

"An ostrich egg is quite large," their guide went on to say. "It can be as much as six inches long and weighs up to three and a half pounds."

Dan looked at Mark, and his eyes grew wide. "Can you imagine what a big plate of scrambled eggs just one ostrich egg would make?"

Mark chuckled. "Or how 'bout a ham and cheese omelet?"

Everyone in the wagon, including Dan's parents and their guide, got a good laugh out of that.

"In this next area there will be more animals roaming around us," their guide said. "You'll have to watch again because some of the animals will get pretty excited when they come up to the wagon looking for something to eat."

Mark and Dan looked at each other with anticipation. *Could this tour get any more exciting?* Mark wondered. He hardly knew which way to look—to the left or right? There were animals everywhere: llamas, fallow deer, and even a few more zebras. Mark loved the little fallow deer. They all had spots and looked like the baby white-tailed fawns they often saw in the fields near his home each spring.

The driver stopped the wagon so some of the people

could take photos. Mark still had some feed left in his bucket, and when he saw two llamas approach, he put some in his hand, just like the guide had instructed, and held it out to them. At first the llamas ate from his hand, but those llamas were smart and knew more feed was in the bucket, so they came in closer. The bigger one stuck his nose right into the container Mark had been holding, nearly knocking it out of his hands.

"Hey, watch it there, boy!" Mark giggled as the other llama tried to stick his head in the same bucket. "You'll have to take your turn."

When the smaller llama tried again to eat from the bucket, the bigger one wanted no part of it. All of a sudden it spit toward the smaller one, but unfortunately its aim wasn't the best.

"Ewww. . ." Mark made a face, setting his bucket down on the floor of the wagon and wiping at the front of his shirt. "He spit on me!"

Dan laughed, and the rest on the wagon joined in, even Mark. "Well, guess that ol' llama was just tryin' to let everyone know who was the boss."

"You're right about that." Their guide chuckled and handed Mark a paper towel. "I keep these towels on the wagon just for occasions like this. See, llamas usually spit at each other to show dominance, but sometimes they do spit at humans. Unfortunately," he added, "you just happened to be in the line of fire."

As they rode up over the hill to the fenced-in area ahead, Mark couldn't help chuckling to himself and wondering how Mattie would have reacted with that llama spitting so close. Shaking his head, he could only imagine.

"Now we're coming to the place where the giraffes are kept," the guide announced. "They're kept in here because we can't have them roaming all over the place. Now, when we stop, they'll stick their long necks over the fence so we can feed them."

"Look how big they are!" Dan's sister, Becky, exclaimed.

Mark snickered when one of the larger giraffes gobbled up the rest of the food in his bucket. It was exciting to see them up close like this and actually be able to pet them.

After the tour, Mark was surprised when Dan's dad said, "Come on kids, we're not done yet. Now we're going to have a picnic."

Dan and Mark looked in the direction where Dan's dad was pointing. "Over there's the picnic area, and that's where we'll have our lunch."

Dan's mom had a picnic basket packed with bologna sandwiches, carrots, and celery to munch on; and there was a big bag of potato chips, too. She'd also brought along a large thermos of cold lemonade to drink.

Inside the farmhouse, where people could visit to see what a real Amish home looked like, was an assortment of cookies. So Dan's dad picked up several and said that would be their dessert.

They walked down to an area where there was a rock garden with a waterfall and small pond. There were all kinds of ducks swimming in there, as well as over in the huge pond full of fish by the picnic area.

"Wow, look at this!" Mark yelled to Dan. "We get to walk through a covered bridge to get to the picnic tables."

"I know," said Dan. "Hasn't this day been fun?"

Mark gave a nod. He couldn't wait to tell Mattie about everything he'd seen and done there at the Farm. He was having a really good time on this zoo-rific day. Even the llama spitting on him wasn't that bad. It was a shame his sister couldn't have come. He hoped Mattie wasn't too bored at home.

CHAPTER 6

Selfish Decisions

"I had so much fun at the Farm the other day," Mark said to Mattie as they rode their bike home from school on Monday afternoon. "Some of those animals were extraordinary!"

Mattie frowned. She knew what extraordinary meant, since Mark had used that word before, but she didn't want to be reminded of how much fun he'd had on Saturday.

"You would have really laughed if you'd seen that llama spit on me," Mark added.

Mattie knew it must have been funny, but hearing about it made her wish all the more that she could have been there to see everything. She turned her head, hearing a familiar *clip-clop*, and waved when she realized the driver was an elderly woman they knew, Freda Hostetler.

"You're awfully quiet back there," Mark called over his shoulder as Freda's horse and buggy went by. "Don't you wanna hear about all the unusual animals I saw?"

"You already told me about some of them."

"I know, but there's more that I didn't tell ya."

"Maybe later," Mattie said. "Right now we need to think about gettin' home."

Mattie knew her brother was excited to tell her more about the trip to the Farm with Dan's family. Actually, she was curious to hear about it but still felt a bit annoyed that she didn't get to go along. At least her brother was nice enough to bring home a few cookies for her, though. It was really his dessert, but he'd said he felt bad for Mattie and had brought the treat home for her instead of eating the cookies himself.

"I'm anxious to get home, too," Mark said. "I need to ask Mom a question."

"What's that?"

"My best friend, John Schrock, invited me to go over to his house to play on Saturday, and I need to ask Mom if it's okay."

"I thought you were supposed to go fishing with Grandpa on Saturday."

"I was, but I'd rather go over to John's house and play. He has a new pony, and I'm eager to see how well it pulls John's pony cart."

"Grandpa might be disappointed if you don't go fishing with him," Mattie said.

Mark shook his head. "I don't think he will care. Calvin's planning to go fishing, too, so Grandpa shouldn't mind if I don't go along. Besides, I can go with Grandpa some other time. Ike's not going either," he added, rolling his eyes. "He's goin' hiking with friends, and I'll bet Catherine's goin', too."

Mattie didn't say anything—just kept pedaling the bicycle. She was pretty sure that Grandpa would be disappointed since the fishing had already been set, and she didn't think it was right that Mark had changed his mind about going, even if Ike did have other plans. After all, he could go to John's house some other time.

❖

On Saturday morning, after Mark left for John's house, Mom and Mattie did the breakfast dishes. When they were just finishing up, Mom turned to Mattie and said, "There's something else I need you to do."

"What's that?" Mattie asked.

"When I went out to the phone shack to check for phone messages this morning, there was one from Grandma Miller. She said she's out of flour and asked if I had some she could borrow. Since Grandpa took their horse and buggy to the pond to go fishing, Grandma has no way of getting to the store to buy more flour." Mom paused and let the water out of the sink. "So I called her back and left a message, saying I would send you over with the flour as soon as we finished doing the breakfast dishes."

Mattie frowned. She didn't feel like walking all the way to Grandma's, and it would be too hard to ride the bicycle built for two without Mark's help. Besides, now that the dishes were done, she'd hoped to spend the rest of the day teaching Twinkles some new tricks, and maybe afterward she would play with the paper dolls she and Mom had made when Mattie was sick.

"Does Grandma need the flour right now?" Mattie asked. "Can't it wait till Grandpa gets home?"

"She's doing some baking this morning, so it really can't wait." Mom took a sack of flour from the cupboard and handed it to Mattie. "If you want to stay and visit with

Grandma awhile, that's fine with me."

Mattie shook her head. "I want to teach Twinkles some new tricks, so I'll come right home after I give Grandma the flour."

Mom shrugged. "If that's what you want, but I'm sure Grandma would enjoy your company. You might even be treated to some of her appeditlich kichlin if you stay awhile."

"I know her cookies are delicious, and maybe I'll stay some other time," Mattie said. "I just don't feel like visiting today." She turned and opened the back door.

"Take your time and don't run," Mom instructed. "It wouldn't be good if you dropped the flour."

"I'll be careful," Mattie called as she stepped onto the porch. She wouldn't run to Grandma's, but she would walk fast. The sooner she got there, the sooner she could come home.

And the sooner she got home, the sooner she could teach Twinkles some new tricks.

Scattered leaves crunched beneath Mattie's feet as she trudged along the path between their house and Grandma and Grandpa Miller's. A flock of geese, flying in a perfect V formation, flew directly overhead, honking as they went, but Mattie didn't take the time to look at them. She didn't even stop to pick any of the wildflowers growing along the path. She just continued to walk at a very fast pace.

Finally, Grandma and Grandpa's large white house came into view. Mattie hurried up the steps and knocked on the door. A few seconds later, Grandma, wearing the apron she always wore whenever she did any baking or chores, opened the door.

"It's good to see you, Mattie," she said, smiling and giving Mattie a warm, affectionate hug. "I see that you brought me some flour."

"Jah." Mattie stepped into the kitchen and handed the sack to Grandma, then she turned to go.

"Don't rush off," Grandma said. "Wouldn't you like to stay and help me bake some chocolate chip kichlin?"

"Maybe another time," Mattie said. "I need to get home so I can teach Twinkles some new tricks."

"Oh, I see." Grandma's smile faded. Even her dark brown eyes looked sad.

"I'll come over another time and help you bake," Mattie said, hoping to make Grandma feel a bit better.

"I'll look forward to that." Grandma set the sack of flour on the kitchen table. "I'll just take out what I need for my baking projects, and you can take the rest of the flour home to your mamm."

"Okay." Mattie waited while Grandma poured some of the flour into a large mixing bowl; then Grandma handed her the sack of flour.

"Danki for bringing this to me." Grandma's smile was back, so Mattie figured Grandma wasn't too upset about her going home.

"See you at church tomorrow," Mattie said as she hurried out the door.

"Jah. Have a good rest of the day," Grandma called.

Mattie couldn't wait to get home, so she decided to run all the way. She'd only gone a short distance, however, when she tripped on a broken tree limb and dropped the sack of flour. *Whoosh!*—it broke, spilling flour everywhere. Some of it shot straight up, covering Mattie's blue dress with a coating of white.

"Oh no," Mattie groaned. "I wish now that I'd stayed at Grandma's and done some baking with her." *Serves me right, I guess. That's what I get for being so selfish and wantin' to hurry right home.*

Mattie's conscience sounded almost too familiar, thinking back earlier to what she had almost said to Mark when he'd decided to go to John's house instead of fishing with Grandpa like he'd originally planned. "Guess I could have taught Twinkles some tricks another time," she murmured.

❀

"Wie geht's?" John asked when Mark entered his yard.

"I'm doin' good. How 'bout you?"

John frowned. "I'd be doin' better if my daed would let me hitch Little Ben to the pony cart."

"I thought that's why you got a new pony," Mark said. "Isn't he supposed to pull your pony cart?"

John gave a nod. "That's right, but Dad says Little Ben isn't trained well enough yet, so I'm not allowed to take him out with the cart till Dad works with him some more."

Mark kicked at a rock with the toe of his boot, feeling so disappointed. "I came over here to see the pony and ride in the cart. What are we supposed to do if we can't take him out in the cart?"

John shrugged as he turned his hands up. "We can pet him, I guess."

Mark didn't think petting the pony would be that much fun. He could have stayed home and pet Lucky today or gone fishing with Grandpa. But he didn't want to be rude, so he followed John into the barn to take a look at the pony. They found Little Ben in his stall, sleeping on a pile of straw.

"Let's go inside and pet him," John said, opening the stall gate.

Mark stepped in behind John and knelt on the floor beside the brown and white pony. Little Ben opened one eye when John began to stroke him behind the ear.

"He's a nice-looking pony," Mark said. "Sure wish we could hitch him to the pony cart and go for a ride."

John sighed. "I wish we could, too, but I'd be in big trouble if I disobeyed my daed."

"If we can't take the pony cart out, what can we do today?" Mark asked.

"Why don't we play some ball?"

Mark shook his head. "You know I don't like playing ball."

"How about if we go look for some frogs in the creek behind my house?" John suggested.

"I'm not in the mood to look for frogs," Mark said. "I already have a frog that lives in the little frog house I put in Mattie's flower bed after our last birthday. Besides, it's autumn, and we might not find too many frogs this time of the year."

John tapped the end of his chin with his finger. "I know. . .I'll get out my jar of glickers, and we can play a game with those."

Mark shook his head. "I'd rather not." Just the mention of marbles made Mark think about the big marble Grandpa Troyer had given him that he'd lost in the pile of leaves. He'd looked for it several times after that but hadn't had any luck finding it. He figured the marble was probably gone forever.

"So what do you wanna do?" John asked, shrugging his shoulders.

"I really want to go for a ride in your pony cart. That's why I came over here today, ya know," Mark said.

"Well, we can't. I already told you. . . ."

"I know. . .your daed said Little Ben isn't ready to pull the cart yet."

"That's right, so now let's think of somethin' else we can do that'll be fun."

Mark took a seat on a bale of straw and made little circles across his forehead as he thought and thought. He couldn't think of one single thing he wanted to do, other than going for a ride in John's pony cart.

Mark sat there awhile, and then he stood. "You know, I think it's time for me to go home."

John's dark eyebrows shot way up. "What? You just got here, and we haven't done anything but sit and talk."

Mark released a noisy yawn. "I know, but I'm feelin' kind of tired. Think I'll go home and take a *gern*."

"If you want to take a nap, that's fine with me, because you obviously didn't come over here to play." Mark could tell by the scowl on John's face that he wasn't happy about Mark leaving. But why should he stick around here when he was so bored? Didn't he have the right to go home?

"I'll see you at church tomorrow morning," Mark said. Then he turned and sprinted in the direction of home.

He'd only made it halfway there when that same big black shaggy dog that had caused so much trouble at their stand a few weeks ago came running out of the woods.

Woof! Woof! It chased after Mark, barking and swishing its tail. Mark didn't know if the dog was mean or just wanted to play, but he didn't stick around to find out. Panting for breath, he ran even faster. When the dog's barking quieted, Mark glanced over his shoulder. He didn't see any sign of the mutt, but he kept running, just in case. Who knew where that dog came from anyway? Surely it couldn't belong to anyone. If it did, then the owners didn't take very good care of their pet.

Mark was nearing his driveway when he tripped on a rock and dropped to the ground. He winced when he saw that the rock he'd fallen on had torn a hole in his trousers and scraped his knee.

Mark clambered to his feet and limped the rest of the way home. He'd just started up the driveway when Calvin came along, swinging his fishing pole and whistling a merry tune. "Grandpa and I both caught plenty of fish today," he said, smiling at Mark. "But I must say, he was disappointed that you didn't come along."

"I wish now that I had," Mark said with a moan. "Instead of takin' a ride in John's pony cart like I'd hope, I ended up with a scraped knee and a hole in my pants!"

Calvin put his hand on Mark's shoulder. "I hope you learned a lesson today. When someone invites you to go someplace and you say you will, then you shouldn't change your mind at the last minute and do something else that you think will be more fun."

Mark gave a quick nod. But then as he thought more about it, he figured if they just could have hitched John's new pony to the cart, he wouldn't be so miserable right now.

When Mark and Calvin stepped onto the porch, Mark was surprised to see Mattie there with splotches of flour all over her dress. "What happened to you?" he asked.

Mattie explained that she'd taken some flour to Grandma, and that even though Grandma had asked her stay, she'd decided to go home. Then as she was carrying the rest of the flour home, she'd tripped and lost the whole bag. "Think I ended up with most of it on me," she muttered, motioning to her dress.

Mark chuckled, and Calvin laughed out loud. "You look like you've been caught in a snowstorm," Calvin said.

"It's not funny." Mattie frowned as she brushed at the flour. Then looking back at Mark, she pointed to the hole in his trousers. "What happened to you?"

"Remember the mutt that caused all the trouble at our roadside stand awhile back?"

Mattie nodded.

"Well, the mutt started chasin' me as I was comin' back from John's, and when I fell, I tore a hole in my trousers." Mark grunted. "Made me wish I'd gone fishin' today instead of goin' over to John's."

"You'd have been better off," Calvin said. "You would have been holdin' a bucket of fish right now if you had." He looked first at Mark and then at Mattie. "You both might have had a better day if you'd thought of others instead of yourselves."

CHAPTER 7

Walnut Juice

The following Saturday turned out to be a pretty autumn day, so Dad announced during breakfast that morning that today was going to be their yearly walnut-picking day. Every year in the fall, one of the many things they liked to do as a family was to gather nuts for the upcoming holiday baking season. Luckily, there happened to be a black walnut tree a little ways down the road in a meadow between the Millers' place and the Shrocks'. Since Mark and his best friend, John Schrock, had walked back and forth to and from each other's home whenever they met to play, Mark knew exactly where that walnut tree was. He also knew after the last time he'd been to John's that the tree was loaded with walnuts this year. Some were on the ground, and some still clung to the branches.

Mark and Mattie loved to pick walnuts with their family and looked forward to it every autumn. Mark knew that Mattie preferred to wear the gloves Mom would hand out to keep fingers clean, but Mark liked to get his fingers all stained from the walnuts' juice. Not all the walnuts still had the green hull on the outer layer. As the black walnuts ripened, the husks changed from solid green to yellowish green, and the skins softened, sometimes leaking the dark liquid from inside. Those were the ones you had to watch out for when you went to pick them up.

As soon as breakfast was over, the whole family, except for Ike, headed out. Ike had gone to his girlfriend Catherine's house today to help her family make apple butter. Mom had packed a bunch of paper bags and put them in her canvas satchel, and when they reached the old walnut tree, she handed each family member a paper sack.

"Make sure, now," Dad instructed, "that you don't overload your bag and make it too heavy to lift. Only pick as many walnuts as you can carry home."

Even little Ada was old enough this year to get in on the act. This was a new experience for her, and she was so excited to help pick the nuts, along with her older brothers and sister, that she kept waving her hands and hollering, "*Walnuss!* Walnuss!"

"Look at all these walnuts!" Mattie exclaimed, pointing at the ones scattered all over the ground. "There must be over a hundred of 'em layin' here, and that's not countin' the ones still hanging on the branches."

"I remember last year this tree didn't produce nearly as many walnuts, but I read that there are usually two good nut crops out of every five years," Dad said, bending over to pick up some walnuts.

"That's interesting," Mattie said as she began filling her sack. "I'm surprised the squirrels haven't taken any of these yet."

"Did ya know that black walnut trees can live to be over two hundred years old?" Mark announced.

"Well, this one must be at least fifty years old 'cause

just look how tall it is!" Mattie tipped her head way back and stared up at the tree. "I'll bet if we climbed up to that highest branch, we could see all of Walnut Creek from up there."

"Now don't get any ideas about climbing the tree," Mom warned. "That could be dangerous."

"I know this tree has to be over ten years old 'cause that's when they start producing nuts," Mark said. "And look how many years we've been comin' here to collect 'em."

"How do you know all this stuff about walnut trees?" Calvin asked. He, too, didn't wear gloves, and his fingers were already turning a brown stain color.

"I read a lot," Mark answered. "If ya ever wanna know something about anything, just ask 'cause I might have read about it and can answer your questions."

"That's right, I forgot you're the curious one in the family," Russell teased, lifting Mark's straw hat off his head and then flopping it back down.

"Hey now, there's nothing wrong with wanting to learn about things," Dad said, joining the boys on the other side of the tree.

"And you are never too old to ask questions about something either," Mom added, watching as Ada put another walnut into her bag.

Mark stopped to watch little Ada, too. She sure looked like she was having fun filling up her bag with walnuts. Each one she picked up she'd say, "Look, Mamm. I found another walnuss!"

"I found one that's open, and look here. . .there's a white worm inside!" Perry announced, looking rather pleased with himself.

"Just toss it aside," Dad said. "We don't want any wormy nuts."

Perry looked a bit disappointed, but he did as Dad asked.

"I wish Ike were here with us," Mark grumbled to Mattie as they continued to fill their bags with nuts. "He's missin' out on all the family fun just to be with Catherine." Mark had always looked up to his big brother. The last couple of years Ike had paid special attention to Mark, and they'd gotten especially close. At least they had until he'd started seeing Catherine. This was the first year Ike hadn't joined the family to pick walnuts.

Mattie leaned down and wiped the dark stain from a walnut on the meadow grass. "Good thing I'm wearing somethin' on my hands. Look how my gloves are getting stained already."

"I like the stain." Mark held up his black hands and grinned.

"You would—you're a boy."

Ignoring the remark, Mark thought about Ike again and wondered, *What's so great about making apple butter? This is more fun anyways.*

❖

When they got home later that day, Dad instructed everyone to empty their bag of walnuts into the wheelbarrow that was still sitting at the back of the house from the leaf-raking cleanup. Until most of the leaves fell off the branches, raking and picking them up was an ongoing project during the months of autumn, but now, with only a leaf or two still hanging on, and all the rest of the leaves gathered up, the wheelbarrow could be used for something else.

"Mark, after you wash up and change your clothes," Dad said, "I'd like you to push the wheelbarrow into the barn so I can put the walnuts in a big tub of water."

"Okay, Dad," Mark replied, walking into the house. He remembered from years past and from reading about it, that floating the walnuts in water was an easy way to separate the hulls from the hard shell inside. The hulls would float, but the nuts wouldn't. Mark had also heard that some English folks spread the walnuts out on a driveway, and when they drove over the nuts with their vehicles, it quickly shelled off the hulls.

"Hey, Mattie," Mark yelled across the hall from his room. "Do ya wanna help me push the wheelbarrow into the barn when I go back outside?"

"No, that's okay. I'm gonna stay here and play with my *bopp*."

Mark went downstairs wondering why his sister would want to spend such a nice day inside playing with her doll. But then, he wasn't a girl so he couldn't really understand why Mattie did many things that he would never do.

Once outside, he walked to the back of the house where the wheelbarrow sat, now full of walnuts. He was about ready to take them over to the other side of the house where the barn was when he noticed something hopping by his foot. Looking down, he spotted a frog.

Oh wow, he thought. *That sure looks like a wood frog to me. I never expected to see any frogs this time of year.*

The wood frog was a brownish-tan frog, and it was easy to tell what kind it was because of the bandit-looking patch that extended from its nose and across its eyes, almost giving it a raccoon look. Mark thought it was so amazing when he'd once learned that wood frogs are capable of freezing completely solid to survive the winter. During this period, the frog's breathing, blood flow, and heartbeat actually stop. And unlike most other frogs, the wood frog spends almost its entire life on the ground. In the winter, it hibernates by burrowing under the ground.

"I've just gotta catch that frog," Mark said as he watched it hop away. He thought it would be great to put the frog in his toad house. Maybe the critter would burrow under the toad house and hibernate this winter in "Mattie's Corner." He couldn't wait to tell Mattie that a frog might be spending the winter in her flower bed, but first he'd have to catch that old bandit-looking frog.

❀

That evening after dark when everyone was sitting in the living room, the Miller family enjoyed talking about the fun day they'd had together.

Calvin, Russell, and Mark compared their fingers to see whose had gotten the most walnut stained. Mattie, rolling her eyes at her brothers, was glad that her fingers were still nice and clean.

"How'd the walnut picking go today?" Ike asked when he returned from Catherine's that evening.

"Real well," Dad answered. "We got a lot of nuts we can use during the winter months."

"And how was your day, Ike?" Mom asked.

"It was great! As you know, Catherine is the youngest of the four *kinner* in her family. And since she's the only girl, her three older brothers were keeping an eye on me. Not that they had to, though." Ike chuckled. "Anyways, it was interesting to help Catherine's family make apple butter."

Mom smiled. "I enjoy making apple butter, too, and let's not forget the apple cider."

"Say, Mark," Dad said. "Did you put the walnuts in the barn like I asked you to when we got home this afternoon?"

"Uh-oh!" Mark slapped his forehead. "I went out to do that, but I found this neat-looking wood frog. It took me awhile to catch the critter 'cause it kept hoppin' away from me. Then when I did finally catch it, I put it in the toad house in Mattie's garden."

Mark proceeded to tell his family all about wood frogs until Dad interrupted him and said, "Well, son, that's interesting, but I want you to make sure you get those walnuts moved into the barn first thing tomorrow morning."

"Sorry I forgot, Dad. I promise I'll take care of it as soon as I'm up and dressed."

CHAPTER 8

Copycat

Before eating breakfast on Monday morning, Mark suddenly remembered that he hadn't moved the wheelbarrow into the barn the day before. Since that had been their off-Sunday from church and they'd gone to visit Grandpa and Grandma Miller, he'd completely forgotten about the wheelbarrow full of nuts. Knowing he'd better take care of that right now, he dashed out the back door so he could get the walnuts into the barn before heading off to school.

As Mark went around the corner of the house, he noticed a squirrel running across the yard and onto the fence railing along their field. It looked like the animal had something in its mouth, but Mark didn't think anything of it—until he got to the wheelbarrow.

"Oh no!" Mark put his hands on his head and stared at the few walnuts that were left. "Where are all the walnuts we picked Saturday?" Then slowly, he lifted his gaze to the bushy-tailed varmint making its getaway into the highest oak tree on the other side of the fence.

After putting the few walnuts that were left in the barn, Mark went into the house, not sure how to tell his parents about the newly discovered backyard thief. If only he'd put those walnuts in the barn yesterday.

"Did you get the walnuts moved?" Dad asked when Mark and the others sat down to breakfast.

"Uh. . .no. . . . Well, a few," Mark stammered. "See, I—uh—forgot to move the wheelbarrow into the barn yesterday morning, so a few minutes ago I went out to do what you'd asked me to do, and I saw this squirrel." Mark swallowed hard. "Dad, that varmint stole almost all the walnuts and only left us a few. I saw him runnin' toward the trees on the other side of our fence with one of the walnuts in his mouth."

Dad cleared his throat real loud, and Mark sat there waiting with his eyes squeezed shut for the scolding he knew would soon come. Then, to his surprise, Mom and Dad burst out laughing.

Mark opened his eyes and looked quizzically at his parents. They laughed so hard that Mom had tears running down her cheeks and Dad's beard jiggled up and down.

Mark looked over at Mattie to see her reaction, but she just shrugged her shoulders and started giggling.

After Mom and Dad finally stopped laughing, Dad looked at Mark and said, "Well, son, it doesn't excuse the fact that you should have done what I asked you to do with the walnuts right away. If you wouldn't have been thinking of that frog and trying to catch him instead of doing what you were told to do, our bushy-tailed friend wouldn't have stolen all the walnuts we picked."

"You're right, Dad, and I'm sorry." Mark hung his head, feeling pretty bad that all the work that had gone into picking the walnuts had gone to waste.

"But we can't blame the squirrel for finding an easy source of food for the winter." Mom smiled. "In case you're wondering, your daed and I were laughing because something similar happened to us when we were first married. We had a whole wagon full of walnuts that we'd just picked, and by mistake we left them in the wagon because we'd gotten busy doing something else that day. Only our story ends a bit differently."

"That's right," Dad said. "When we went out the next morning, the wagon was totally empty, and there was not one walnut to be found." Dad gave Mark's shoulder a squeeze. "Don't you worry, son, we had a good time Saturday having family time together, and there are plenty more walnuts left where we picked those. So, Mark, maybe you can convince one of your brothers or Mattie to go along with you to pick some more nuts after school."

"I'll go with you," Ike quickly volunteered. "Since I missed out on Saturday's walnut picking, I'd be glad to help you get more."

Mark was happy that Dad wasn't too upset and that he'd be doing something fun with his big brother Ike. He'd also learned a good lesson, though, about doing what he was told to do instead of what he wanted to do.

❀

"You're tryin' to cram too much in," Mattie mumbled when Mark put a big, thick book in the basket on their bike before they left for school. "What is that, anyway?"

"It's my dictionary," Mark said. "I'm gonna study it during recess today so I can have some new big words to say."

Mattie frowned. "You don't need any more big words to say. You've said enough of those already." She stuffed her jump rope into the basket beside her lunch pail. "And you shouldn't be taking up room in our basket with that big book."

"If you think it's too crowded, then why don't you take your jump rope out?" Mark asked.

She shook her head. "My jump rope hardly takes up any room at all, and I'm takin' it so some of the girls and I can have fun jumping during recess."

Mark shrugged. "That's fine by me. Let's just get going or we're gonna be late."

Mattie climbed onto the back of the bike, and Mark climbed onto the front. As they pedaled out of the yard, a cool breeze came up, swirling some of the fallen leaves into the air.

Mattie shivered. Fall was definitely here, and she was glad she'd worn a jacket today. From the looks of the gray sky overhead, it could even rain before the day was out. She hoped no rain would fall—at least not until they were home from school. It was never fun to be caught in the drenching rain, even though they no longer had to walk since they'd been given a bike.

They were halfway to the schoolhouse when they hit a bump and Mattie's jump rope bounced out. The next thing she knew the bike had come to a complete stop. Mattie pumped her legs and pushed her feet hard against the pedals, but she couldn't get them to move forward or back.

"What's going on?" Mark called over his shoulder. "The bike's not moving. Did you stop pedaling, Mattie?"

"No, I did not. My jump rope fell out, and I think it

might be stuck in the chain."

Mark got off the bike and squatted down beside the chain. "Jah, that's what happened, all right. Now we need to figure out how to get the jump rope loose."

Mattie got off, set the kickstand, and knelt on the ground next to Mark.

First, Mark pulled on the jump rope, and then Mattie gave it a try. It was such a tangled mess she didn't think they'd ever get it out.

"Be careful, Mattie," Mark said. "If we pull too hard, we might break the chain."

"What are we gonna do?" she asked, feeling a sense of panic.

"Just keep trying to get it off."

They both twisted and pulled and twisted some more. Suddenly, the chain popped right off!

"That's just great," Mark mumbled. "Now we're gonna have to push the bike the rest of the way to school."

"If we do that, we'll be late," Mattie said. "Can't we just leave the bike here and run the rest of the way?"

Mark shook his head. "If we leave the bike, someone might steal it. Then we'll be walking to school from now on instead of ridin' our bike."

Mattie's lips compressed as she gave Mark's words some serious thought. "You're right. It wouldn't be good if someone stole our bicycle. Guess we'd better start pushing, even if it does make us late."

❁

When the twins entered the schoolhouse, their teacher, Anna Ruth Stutzman, looked at Mark and Mattie and said,

"You two are late."

"We're sorry," the twins both said.

"We had a little problem with the chain on our bike," Mark explained. "We ended up havin' to push the bike the rest of the way to school."

"I'm sorry to hear that. Now please take your seats."

Mark's face heated with embarrassment. Mattie's cheeks were red, too. All the other scholars seemed to be looking at them.

They'd just taken their seats when Anna Ruth took out her Bible. "This morning I'll be reading from First Thessalonians 5:18: 'Give thanks in all circumstances; for this is God's will for you in Christ Jesus.' "

Mark sat at his desk, mulling things over. Was he supposed to feel thankful that their bike chain had fallen off and they'd been late for school? It was a lot easier to be thankful when things went well, but he did want to do what the Bible said.

"I know it's not always easy to be thankful when things don't go as we'd like," Anna Ruth said as though she knew what Mark was thinking. "But if we have an attitude of thankfulness, it helps us deal with things better. After all, it doesn't do any good to get mad when things go wrong. When we go through hard times, it can actually help to strengthen our character."

Mark glanced over at Mattie to see her reaction, but she was whispering something to her friend Stella.

Next the teacher told the children to stand and recite the Lord's Prayer. Following that, everyone filed to the front of the room and sang a few songs.

Mark didn't feel much like singing today, but he forced

himself to do it. He couldn't stop thinking about the bike and wondering what Dad would say when they told him what had happened.

After the singing, everyone took their seats, and Anna Ruth gave the arithmetic assignment. When that was done, she told the class that they had another assignment to do.

"I'd like you to write an essay, either about something you've recently learned to do or something that's taught you about becoming responsible. This assignment will be due by the end of the week, and everyone will get the chance to read what they wrote to the class."

I wonder what I should write about, Mark thought. *Whatever topic I choose, I think I'll include a big word or two.*

❀

"I can't think of anything to write about," Mattie told Mark as they pushed their bike home from school that afternoon. "What topic are you gonna choose?" she asked.

"I think I'll write about how we learned to ride our bicycle built for two," Mark said. "It was a real challenge for us at first, remember?"

"Jah, I sure do." Mattie sighed. "I can't think of anything to write about. Do you have any ideas for me?"

Mark stopped pushing the bike and turned to face her. "Anna Ruth said we could write about something that has taught us to be responsible. Maybe you could write about all the things you do to care for Twinkles. Takin' care of our pets has taught us both about responsibility."

"I guess you're right. Besides feeding and watering

Twinkles, I'm responsible for brushing her hair and teaching her tricks." Mattie smiled. "Jah, I think I will write about that. Danki, Mark, for giving me the idea."

He grinned at her. "You're welcome."

❧

Mattie was glad that Dad had been able to get the jump rope untangled and put the chain back on their bike. That meant she and Mark could ride to school again. She was also glad she had until the end of the week to get her essay done, and she spent every evening that week working on it. Putting words together in the form of an essay wasn't something she enjoyed, but at least she had an interesting topic to write about. She was glad Mark had suggested it and hoped she'd get a good grade.

When Friday came and the twins went to school, Mattie became nervous. She dreaded reading her essay in front of the class. And what if the teacher didn't like what she'd written?

Mattie had a hard time concentrating at the beginning of class as they recited the Lord's Prayer, sang some songs, and listened to the teacher read a verse of scripture.

After their arithmetic lesson was over, Anna Ruth told everyone to get out their essays and said they would take turns reading them.

Mattie's heart started to race. *I hope she doesn't call on me first. If she does, though, at least I'll be getting it over with. Then I can relax and listen to everyone else read their essay.*

Anna Ruth looked at Mark and gave him a nod. "You have an eager look on your face, so why don't you go first?"

Good, Mattie thought. *At least I don't have to be first.*
Mattie had never liked speaking in front of the class.
It made her stomach knot up and turned her hands all
sweaty. She was afraid she might say something dumb.
Mark didn't have a problem with talking in front of the
class, though. He always seemed calm and relaxed.

Mattie leaned forward, anxious to hear what Mark had
written about riding their bike. *This should be really good*,
she thought. That bicycle built for two had taught them a
lot about working together as a team—not just with riding
the bike but in many other ways, too. It was a good topic
for Mark to write about, and she was sure he'd have a lot
to say on the subject. She just hoped he wouldn't mention
some of the silly mistakes she'd made when they'd first
begun learning to ride the bike. Letting their whole class
know about that would really be embarrassing for Mattie.

Mark picked up his paper and went to the front of the
class. "The name of my essay is: How I Take Care of My
Pets."

Mattie's mouth dropped open. *What? Now, wait
a minute! I thought Mark was going to write about
learning to ride our bicycle built for two. He told me
to write about caring for my pet, but then he went and
wrote about it. What a copycat my brother is!*

"Caring for my cat, Lucky, involves a lot of
responsibility, and I'm the one who has to take care of
her needs," Mark said. "I'm also responsible for taking
care of Lucky's kitten, Boots. Most kittens are curious,
playful, and energetic, and Boots is all of those things." He
chuckled. "It's fun to watch Boots grow and mature.

"An adult cat, like Lucky, requires less care than my

kitten does," Mark went on to say. "But I don't mind 'cause I enjoy taking care of them both." He paused a minute and smiled at the scholars, who all seemed to be listening intently. "Healthy cats have clear, bright eyes with little or no tearing, and their nostrils and ears are clean. If there's black, tarlike gunk in a cat's ear, it probably means she has ear mites. Lucky had them once, and Dad helped me put medicine in her ears."

Mark is doing such a good job telling about his cat, Mattie thought. *My essay is boring compared to his. I wish he'd chosen something else to write about. He'll probably get a better grade than me, too.*

Looking around the classroom, Mattie could see that her brother had everyone's attention. From the looks she saw on their faces, she knew they were eager to hear more.

"Cats are naturally fastidious," Mark continued. "So I always make sure my cats have fresh food and water and that their dishes are clean. Cats don't like food that is old or water that's stale."

"What's fas-tid-ious mean?" Aaron Stutzman wanted to know.

"It means they like to be clean," Mark said with a wide grin.

Mattie wondered if he was trying to show everyone how smart he was by using such a big word. She gripped the edge of her desk with both hands. It figured that Mark would have to do that!

"You shouldn't ask questions or speak out of turn," Anna Ruth said, looking sternly at Aaron. "If you have a question, please raise your hand." She nodded at Mark. "You may continue reading."

"I always brush my cats regularly so that their hair is shiny and sleek. Cats like to lick themselves: their paws, their legs, their back, and even their tail, which is how they keep clean. By brushing their coat and gettin' the loose fur removed, this also helps the cats not to end up with hair balls. In addition, brushin' the cats' hair helps me to check for fleas." Mark glanced at Mattie but then quickly looked away.

He probably knows I'm upset because he took my topic to write about, she fumed. *Well, why wouldn't I be upset? He was selfish to do that, and I hope he knows it.*

"Taking care of a pet requires love and patience," Mark said. "Cats can be one of the most lovable and playful pets to have. I'm glad I have some pets that have taught me about responsibility." Mark smiled at the teacher and took his seat.

Anna Ruth looked at Mattie then. "Would you like to go next?"

Mattie's heart felt like it had sunk all the way to her toes. Speaking in front of the class was bad enough; having to read the essay she'd written about caring for her pet, after Mark had read his, was horrible! Yet she knew she had to do it, or she wouldn't get a good grade. And if she said no to the teacher, she'd be in big trouble, too.

Drawing in a deep breath, Mattie picked up her paper and slowly made her way to the front of the room. Turning around and looking out at the class, she saw that all eyes were on her now. Mattie's stomach felt queasy, and her mouth turned dry. *Here goes nothing*, she thought. "The name of my essay is: How I Take Care of My Pet," she said, swallowing hard and barely able to speak.

She glanced at Mark, and he smiled at her. Didn't he feel the least bit guilty?

"Please continue, Mattie," Anna Ruth said.

Mattie cleared her throat and wiped one sweaty hand on the side of her dress. "Uh. . . I have a dog named Twinkles, and she's a fox terrier. Caring for her involves a lot of responsibility." She paused and moistened her lips with the tip of her tongue. "The things I do for my dog are: feeding her, giving her fresh water, playing games like 'fetch the ball,' and I also brush her hair at least once a week. That way she doesn't shed so much."

Mattie's cheeks burned. Her essay wasn't nearly as well written as Mark's. She was sure everyone in the class was bored because a couple of the boys were yawning. It was hard to concentrate on reading her essay with so many pairs of eyes watching her, too. *Maybe it would be best if I hurry through it so I can return to my seat and be done with this assignment*, she decided.

"I've taught Twinkles to sit, roll over, and fetch," Mattie said, glad that her essay was finally coming to a close. "My dog's very smart, and someday I'll teach her to jump through a hoop." Red-faced and feeling more nervous than ever, Mattie turned to the teacher and said, "That's all I have."

"Very well, you may return to your seat," Anna Ruth said.

Mattie sank into the chair at her desk, wishing she could crawl right under it and stay there for the rest of the day. It had felt like forever, standing there in front of the whole class, and it was all Mark's fault that her essay wasn't as good as his. If he just hadn't chosen the same topic, maybe the things she'd written wouldn't have sounded so boring.

As Mattie's friend Stella got up to read her essay, Mattie looked up at the sign on the wall above the teacher's desk. It read: YOU ARE RESPONSIBLE FOR YOU.

Mattie blinked against the tears stinging her eyes. *I should have never asked for Mark's help. I should have chosen a topic to write about myself. Next time I'll know better.*

Chapter 9

Horse Sense

"Can I play with your *gaul*?" Mark's little brother, Perry, asked when he entered Mark's bedroom.

Mark's gaze went to the small wooden horse sitting on his dresser across the room. Dad had carved it and given the toy to Mark for Christmas last year. That made it very special.

"No," Mark said. "You can't play with my wooden gaul."

Perry's bottom lip jutted out. "*Sei net so* eegesinnisch."

"I'm not being selfish. I just don't want you to play with it."

"How come?"

"Because you might break it."

Perry shook his head. "Huh-uh. I'll be *achtsam*."

"You might think you're being careful, but you're not old enough to play with something so fragile."

"Sei net so eegesinnisch," Perry mumbled as he lowered his head and shuffled out of the room.

Mark knew his little brother was upset, but he figured Perry would get over it as soon as he found something else to do. *Besides, the horse is mine, and I don't have to let Perry play with it if I don't want to*, he thought. Mark leaned against his pillows and went back to reading his book.

A few minutes later, Mattie poked her head into the room. "I just talked to Perry, and he said you're *eegesinnisch*. How come he said you were selfish, Mark?" she asked.

"He wanted to play with the little wooden horse Dad gave me last Christmas, and I said no because he might break it."

"I don't blame you for saying no," Mattie said. "Remember awhile back what happened when Ada got ahold of my bopp?"

Mark gave a nod. "Jah, she scribbled on the doll's face with black ink."

"That's right, and now it's her doll to play with." Mattie frowned. "I sure didn't want the bopp after that, and I was glad when my friend Stella gave me a new one for my birthday."

"If I'd let Perry play with my gaul and he broke it, Dad probably wouldn't have time to make me a new one. He and Ike have been keepin' real busy in the wood shop lately."

"Do you think you'll work for Dad in the wood shop after you graduate the eighth grade?" Mattie asked.

Mark shrugged. "Maybe, but I don't really know yet what I wanna do. How 'bout you, Mattie? Do you know what you want to do when you finish school?"

"I'm not sure. One thing I know is that I don't wanna teach school."

"How come?"

"I'm too *dumm*."

"You're not dumb, Mattie. You just need to study harder and not daydream so much."

"I can't help it. There are so many things I like to think about."

"Well, you oughta save your daydreamin' for nighttime when you're in bed."

"I can't do that," Mattie said with a quick shake of her head. "Some thoughts just pop into my mind at any old time of the day." She moved closer to Mark's bed. "What's that buch you're reading?"

"It's a book about all different kinds of keffer. I'm studying it so I can name all the ones I find in our yard."

Mattie wrinkled her nose. "I can think of lots of better things to do than study bugs."

"Well, you like flowers, and I like bugs. That just shows how different we are." Mark chuckled. "But that's what makes us so unique."

"I guess you're right about that." Mattie turned toward the door. "Enjoy your buch about keffer, Mark. I'm goin' outside to play with my hund."

After Mattie left the room, Mark started thinking more about Perry wanting to play with the wooden horse. *Maybe it would be a good idea to hide that horse*, Mark thought. *Just in case Perry decides to sneak into my room when I'm not here and help himself to the toy. Jah, that's what I'll do*, he finally decided. *I'll take the horse and hide it in the barn.*

❀

"Come here, Twinkles," Mattie called after she'd brought the dog's brush out of the house and taken a seat on the top porch step.

Arf! Arf! Twinkles responded with a wag of her stubby tail. Then she raced across the yard, leaped onto the porch, and put her front paws on Mattie's chest.

"Are you excited about getting your hair brushed?" Mattie asked.

Woof! Twinkles gave Mattie a slurpy kiss with a swipe of her little pink tongue.

Mattie giggled; then she made Twinkles lie in her lap so she could brush her smooth brown and white hair. Twinkles was a good dog and did what Mattie said. Mattie was glad Twinkles liked to be brushed.

Brushing Twinkles made Mattie think about the essay she'd written last week and how Mark had chosen the same topic. Mattie was still upset about the fact that he'd gotten a better grade than she did, but at least the teacher had given her a C. The way Mark had written his essay was a lot more interesting than what Mattie had said. It was longer, with more details, too, so he probably deserved the A he'd gotten.

Pushing those thoughts aside, Mattie concentrated on making Twinkles look good. She brushed and brushed until Twinkles's hair was nice and shiny. By the time she was finished, Twinkles had fallen asleep.

"Wake up, Twinkles, you're all done," Mattie said, leaning her head close to the dog.

Soft little snores came from the dog's mouth, and she didn't even open her eyes.

Mattie had planned to teach Twinkles a new trick today, but since the dog had fallen asleep she didn't want to bother her now. So she just sat, stroking Twinkles's head and daydreaming about roasting marshmallows and drinking hot apple cider. She knew Dad planned to make fresh-squeezed cider soon, and oh, it would taste so wonderfully good. Just thinking about it made her mouth water. Whenever Dad made cider, he usually built a bonfire, and that evening the family would roast hot dogs for supper and enjoy toasted marshmallows for dessert.

Mattie wasn't sure she could ever eat another hot dog after watching what happened to Grandma the day she choked. Mattie did love hot dogs, though, and after that incident, she'd probably remember for the rest of her life to eat slowly and always take small bites, no matter what she was eating.

"Hundli!" Ada hollered when she came out of the house and saw Mattie sitting on the porch steps.

"Twinkles is a hund, not a hundli," Mattie said. "Hundli means puppy, and Twinkles is full-grown."

Ada plopped down on the step beside Mattie. *"Hunnskop."* She pointed to Twinkles's head.

"You're right." Mattie nodded. "That's my dog's head."

Without asking permission, Ada reached over and gave Twinkles a pat.

Twinkles's eyes snapped open. *Arf! Arf!* She licked Ada's hand and then slurped the end of her nose with her little pink tongue.

"Hundli! Hundli!" Ada giggled and waved her hands, the way she always did when she was excited.

Woof! Woof! Twinkles leaped off Mattie's lap and raced into the yard. Ada jumped up and chased after the dog.

"Absatz! Stop!" Mattie shouted. "You're gettin' my hund all worked up!" She wished now she'd never let Ada pet Twinkles.

Twinkles kept running and barking, and Ada kept chasing her, hollering, "Hundli! Hundli!"

Twinkles got so worked up that she dropped to the ground and rolled all around. Now she had streaks of green grass and clumps of dirt in her hair!

Mattie clapped her hands and hollered, "Absatz! Absatz!"

Twinkles ignored her and kept rolling and barking, while Ada excitedly jumped up and down.

"That's just great," Mattie mumbled. "Now I'm gonna have to give Twinkles a bath!"

"What's all the noise about?" Mark asked, stepping out of the barn.

Mattie pointed at Twinkles, still rolling around. "Ada got her all excited, and now I can't get her calmed down."

"I can take care of that in a hurry," Mark said. "I'll just get the hose and—"

"Oh no you don't!" Mattie shook her head. "I'm gonna give Twinkles a bath but not with cold *wasser*. If you'll take Ada inside, I think that will help."

Mark gave a nod. Then he grabbed Ada around her waist and said, "Would ya like a horsey ride?"

"Jah!" Ada grinned up at Mark as she bobbed her head.

"Okay then, climb on my back and put your arms around my neck." Mark bent down, and after Ada had her arms securely around his neck, he grabbed hold of her ankles and stood. "Neigh! Neigh!" Mark shouted as he took off for the house.

Mattie smiled. *That twin brother of mine sure is strong.*

Twinkles calmed down in a hurry after that, so Mattie picked the dog up and carried her to the house. "All right,

Twinkles," she said. "It's time now for your bath!"

❀

That evening after supper, Mark and Mattie had just cleared the dishes off the table when Dad announced that he was going out to the barn to groom their horse. "Gotta have Ginger lookin' good when she pulls our buggy to church tomorrow," he said, grinning widely.

Mom smiled and patted Dad's arm. "Even when we were courting, you liked to have your horse well groomed."

"That's true, and I wouldn't be surprised if that's not the reason you agreed to marry me, Alice."

"No way, Willard," Mom said with a shake of her head. "I married you because you knew how to cook."

Mark leaned against the kitchen counter and waited for Dad's reply. In all his nine years, he didn't think he'd ever seen Dad cook a meal in Mom's kitchen.

Dad tipped his head back, and his deep laughter bounced off the walls. "Well," he said, giving Mom a quick wink, "I have boiled water for your tea a time or two. Does that count as cooking?"

Everyone laughed, even Ada and Perry, although Mark didn't think his little sister and brother really knew what they were laughing about.

"You're absolutely right, Willard," Mom said with a twinkle in her eyes. "Knowing you could boil water is the reason I agreed to become your wife."

"I knew it!" Dad slapped his hand against the table. Then he turned to Mark and said, "Now that we've got that all settled, would you like to come out to the barn and help me groom Ginger?"

Mark didn't hesitate to answer, "Jah." Most times Dad asked Ike, Calvin, or Russell to groom the horse. Since he'd asked Mark this evening, that must mean he thought Mark was responsible enough to help.

Dad tapped Mark's shoulder. "All right then, let's head on out to the barn!"

Mark followed Dad out the door. When they entered the barn, he glanced up at the shelf where he'd put his wooden horse for safekeeping. Perry would never find it there, and even if he did, he wouldn't be able to reach it.

Dad opened Ginger's stall door and had just picked up her currycomb, when Lucky ran into the stall, chasing a mouse.

Suddenly, Ginger whinnied and reared up. Then she bolted out of the stall and raced into the main section of the barn. She kicked up her feet, banging walls and knocking into things. The next thing Mark knew, the shelf near the barn door vibrated, and his little wooden horse dropped to the floor with a thud.

Ginger, still thrashing about, stepped on the toy, and it broke into several pieces!

"Oh no!" Mark gasped. "No more wooden horse."

Dad hollered, "Whoa there! Hold steady, Ginger!"

"She smashed my toy horse," Mark said after Dad had grabbed hold of Ginger's halter.

Dad didn't seem to be listening to Mark. He was too busy looking at Ginger's hoof. "This isn't good," Dad said with a shake of his head. "It's not good at all."

"What's wrong?" Mark asked, leaning close to Dad.

"There's a piece of wood wedged in her hoof, and the wound that resulted in her stepping on that toy horse is bleeding pretty bad." Dad's forehead wrinkled. "Guess I'd better go out to the phone shack and call the vet. Looks like we won't be using Ginger to pull our buggy to church in the morning after all."

Mark swallowed hard. If he hadn't hidden the wooden horse in the barn to keep Perry from playing with it, this never would have happened. Mark wished now that he hadn't been so selfish and would have at least let Perry hold the toy. He hoped Ginger would be okay. The poor horse never would have hurt her foot if it hadn't been for his selfishness. Grandpa Miller probably would have said that Mark needed some horse sense!

CHAPTER 10

A New Treasure

On Monday afternoon, just before school ended for the day, Anna Ruth took a bag of candy from a drawer in her desk. Dan and Becky Yoder's mother had given the candy to the teacher this morning and said she could give each of the scholars a piece before they went home today.

Mattie licked her lips as she eagerly waited for her turn to take a piece of candy from the bag. She hoped there was a strawberry-flavored one.

Mark and Mattie were the last ones in line, and Mark got to the teacher's desk just before Mattie. There was only one piece of candy left, and Mark quickly reached inside the sack, snatching it up.

"Hey, what about me?" Mattie couldn't believe Mark had taken the last piece.

"Oh dear," Anna Ruth said. "I guess there wasn't enough candy for all the scholars." She looked at Mark. "Won't you share your piece of candy with Mattie?"

Mark shook his head. "It's chocolate. Mattie doesn't like chocolate."

Anna Ruth looked at Mattie. "Is that true?"

Mattie nodded. "But I would have taken a piece of

chocolate candy if there'd been another one."

"You want half of this one?" Mark asked, although he didn't look too happy about it.

Mattie shook her head. "No, that's okay; you go ahead."

Mark took the wrapper off the candy and popped it into his mouth before his sister could change her mind. "Yum! This sure is good."

"I'll bring you a piece of candy tomorrow," Anna Ruth told Mattie. "What flavor would you like?"

"Strawberry." Mattie smacked her lips. "I like that kind the best."

"I'll see if I can find some strawberry-flavored candy," Anna Ruth said.

Mattie grinned. "Danki, Teacher." Then she turned and followed Mark out the door.

"I wonder why Dan and Becky's mamm didn't send enough candy to school," Mark said as they climbed on their bicycle built for two. "You'd think she'd know how many scholars there are at our school."

"I'm sure she does," Mattie replied. "She probably just didn't count each one in the bag."

"Oh, you mean their mamm probably *estimated* how many she put in the bag?" Mark further explained that the word *estimate* meant a calculated guess.

Mattie rolled her eyes thinking, *There go those big words again.*

Even though her brother's big words annoyed her most of the time, sometimes Mattie actually found herself using those big words after Mark had explained them to her. She didn't want to admit it to him, but she was learning a whole new vocabulary of words, not only from her brother but also from Grandpa Miller. Mattie thought that someday her twin brother would make a good teacher. Maybe he'd end up teaching at their own schoolhouse here in Walnut Creek instead of working with Dad and Ike in the wood shop, liked he'd talked about sometimes.

❁

As they pedaled out of the school yard, Mark called over his shoulder, "Sure hope Ginger's foot is doing better today. Dad wasn't happy about havin' to call the vet, and I don't think anyone in the family liked havin' to walk to church on Sunday morning 'cause Ginger couldn't pull the buggy."

"I didn't mind walking," Mattie said. "It wasn't raining yesterday, and the nice weather gave me a chance to get a close look at all the colored leaves and pretty fall flowers along the way." She tapped Mark on the shoulder. "Speaking of flowers. . .I see some bright yellow ones up ahead. Let's stop a minute so I can pick some to take home."

Mark grunted. "I'm not stoppin' so you can pick posies."

"They're not posies, and I don't want them for me. I thought it would be nice to give a bouquet to Mom."

"Oh, alright." Mark stopped pedaling, and so did Mattie.

After they'd set the bike's kickstand, Mattie walked into the field where she'd seen the flowers, while Mark looked around for any unusual rocks.

"Hey, Mark!" Mattie hollered from the center of the meadow, twirling around with her arms outstretched. "Look at all this. It's like I'm standin' in an ocean of mustard!"

Mark looked in the direction of his sister's voice. Putting his hand above his eyes to shield them from the sun, he realized that Mattie was standing right in the middle of a field full of goldenrod.

"I'm not sure you should pick that, Mattie," Mark warned. "They do look pretty, but I think it's the same weed that makes Perry *niesse*."

Mattie returned with a few stems of the amber-colored plant and asked Mark if he was sure it was this wildflower that made their little brother sneeze.

"Jah, that's what they call goldenrod. It's a type of weed, and Perry's allergic to it," Mark insisted.

"Allergic?"

Mark explained that Perry had an allergy to goldenrod. Having an allergy meant their little brother had an unusual sensitivity to this plant that was otherwise harmless to others. "When Perry's exposed to the weed, he sneezes," Mark said once again. "Allergies cause some people to have a strong reaction. Other times, it's a mild reaction like sneezin'."

"Well, what am I gonna do now?" Mattie asked. "I really wanted to bring Mom a pretty bouquet of *blumme* today."

Mark looked around, and on the other side of the road, near a small grove of trees in the corner of a pasture, he spotted some flowers.

"Look over there near those trees," he said, pointing. "From here, it looks like asters and all sorts of other wildflowers you might wanna check out."

Mattie looked in that direction, carefully crossed the road, and bounded toward the trees. When she got up to the flowers, she started picking right away—pink, pale blue, violet, and white—there were all sorts of pretty wildflowers growing in that spot.

Mark figured Mom would be pleased with the pretty bouquet Mattie would give to her when they got home, and while his sister picked the flowers, Mark found two small rocks that he liked. One was flat with green stripes running through it. The other one was black and shaped like a duck's head.

Mark put both of them in his pocket; then he continued to look around. Suddenly, his eyes caught a flash of silver.

"Hmm. . .I wonder what that is," he said, bending down for a closer look. He was surprised to discover that it was a small knife, and it looked brand new.

Every boy needs a pocketknife, he thought to himself. *Especially me, since I don't have one yet.*

This pocketknife was very unique. It was silver colored, and there was an eagle etched on the outside. When Mark opened the knife, he noticed some lettering carved in the blade, and it read: Soar high, like an Eagle.

Mark turned the knife over and over again, looking at all the details. *This is the best thing I've ever found*, he thought, smiling to himself.

Mark looked around a bit more, hoping to find some other things lying along the road, until Mattie joined him again with her large bouquet of flowers.

"You were right, Mark." Mattie held up the bouquet. "Mom should really like this one. Look how colorful it is."

"Well, I hope we can get them home safely. Just be careful how you put 'em in the basket," Mark said.

"I will." Mattie walked to the back of their bike, where their lunch pails were tied onto the metal carrier. "I think I still have a paper towel in my lunch pail that I can put in the bottom of the bike's basket. That should get the blumme home without ruining 'em."

Waiting for Mattie to take care of the flowers, Mark slipped his new treasure into his pocket. *Maybe I can learn to carve something with this*, he thought. *I won't try a wooden horse because that would be too hard, but I might be able to carve a toy wagon.*

❀

When Mattie and Mark got home, Mattie couldn't wait to show Mom the pretty flowers she'd picked. Luckily, the paper towel had protected the flowers, and they were still in good shape.

Jumping off the bike and not even waiting for her brother, she bounded up the walkway and into the house, knowing that the flowers should be put into a vase with some water.

"Look, Mom!" Mattie exclaimed, out of breath. "I found some pretty blumme for you today on the way home from school."

"Ach, Mattie, they are so nice." Mom took the flowers from her and went to find a vase. "You really did get an assortment of pretty colors today. Danki very much."

When Mom came back holding a clear vase with scalloped edges, Mattie was pleased that she liked them so much.

"How's this vase?" Mom asked.

Mattie smiled. "That one's my favorite."

"I think I'll put these flowers in the center of our table tonight," Mom said as she snipped the bottoms of the stems and arranged them in the vase. "Don't you think they'll look pretty there?"

Mattie bobbed her head.

"Do you know what type of wildflower these are?" Mom asked, motioning to the purple and pink ones.

"Mark said those kind are called asters," Mattie answered, pointing to the colorful flowers that looked like a daisy.

"Jah, I do recognize them now," Mom said. "Do you know that asters are sometimes called Christmas daisies?"

Mattie thought that was special. She sure loved flowers—and Christmas, too.

"You might not realize it yet," Mom said, "but it'll be memories like this that'll make your appreciation for flowers even more meaningful later in life."

Mattie gave a nod. "I think you might be right."

"You should get the wildflower book Grandpa and Grandma Miller gave you for your birthday in August. Maybe you can identify the other wildflowers that are in the bouquet with the asters," Mom suggested.

"I'm goin' to my room right now to look them up." Mattie was pleased that her grandparents had given her such a wonderful gift this year on her birthday. The book had lots of interesting pictures of flowers and their descriptions. It even told where in the United States each type of flower could be found. It also had a chart showing what season of the year certain wildflowers could be seen. All this would make it easier to identify the wildflowers she'd brought home today.

❁

When the family sat down to eat supper that evening, Mattie was eager to share what she'd learned about the other types of wildflowers she'd picked along with the asters. *I probably should have written my essay on the wildflowers of Ohio*, she thought. *That would have been an easy one for me to write about, and it would have been real interesting, too.*

"Look at the pretty flowers Mattie picked for me on the way home from school today," Mom announced to everyone after their silent prayer and she'd started passing around the food.

"Jah, and Mark told me the ones that look like daisies are called asters," Mattie explained. "Then Mom told me that they're also called Christmas daisies."

Everyone listened intently as Mattie shared this newfound information.

"Did you find out what the other ones are called?" Mom asked winking at Mattie.

"Uh-huh. Those deep purple ones are called ironweed, and the pink ones with the rounded clusters are called joe-pye," Mattie was pleased to announce.

"That's very interesting," Dad said. "How did you get to know all of that?"

"I looked it up in the wildflower book Grandma and Grandpa Miller gave to me on my birthday."

Mattie went on to tell that joe-pye sort of smelled like vanilla. She'd also learned that this particular wildflower had once been used for healing purposes by some Native American tribes. The ironweed was also used as medicine during the 1800s and after the Civil War.

"Plus," Mattie added with a smile, seeing that she had everyone's full attention, "some of our state's most beautiful butterflies, including the monarch and tiger swallowtail, love to flit around joe-pye and sip its nectar."

"What about the Great Spangled Fritillary?" Mark asked. "Remember, we saw one of those the day we sat at the roadside stand."

"That's right, I almost forgot. The book said that one of our common butterflies, which is the Great Spangled Fritillary, loves the joe-pye flower, too." Mattie passed Mark the bowl of macaroni salad. "Danki for reminding me about that one."

Mattie's brothers, and even little Ada, clapped after Mattie's very detailed report on what she'd learned, and Mattie was pleased that her parents nodded their heads in approval.

"It's a good thing I told Mattie not to pick the golden-rod she saw first," Mark said. "She forgot that Perry's allergic to it."

"You're right, he most certainly is." Mom gave Mattie's arm a little pat. "So I'm glad the bouquet you brought me had no goldenrod in it."

✿

After supper Mark headed out to the barn. He was happy to see that Ginger was moving around in her stall and didn't seem to be limping as much. A few more days of resting and she'd be good as new.

Mark was kind of upset that Mattie had gotten so much attention during their meal as she'd told all that information about flowers. *Who cares about blumme anyways?* Mark thought. *I was the one who stopped her from picking the goldenrod. I was also the one who pointed out those other wildflowers that she picked for Mom.*

Guess that's kinda selfish of me, Mark corrected himself. *I really should be happy that my sister enjoyed telling all about the flowers.*

Turning his thoughts to other things, Mark spotted some wood stacked along the wall on the other side of the barn. He didn't think Dad would mind if he took one of the smaller pieces, so he helped himself and took a seat on a bale of straw. Then he removed the pocketknife from his pants' pocket and started to whittle. Mark had never done any wood carving before, but he'd watched Dad and Ike do it many times, and it didn't look that hard. He was sure he could carve the wood down so that it looked like a wagon. After all, most of the hunk of wood he was using was square-shaped, so he'd only have to carve out the round wheels. If he did a good job, he might even try making a small horse like the one that had been broken.

Just wait till I show everyone the little wagon I carved. Mark was excited to get his carving done. He could then prove to everyone that he knew a thing or two, just like Mattie had tonight when she'd shared all that information about wildflowers.

Mark had only been carving a few minutes when the knife slipped and sliced his thumb.

"Ouch! Ouch!" It really hurt, and Mark winced when he saw blood oozing from the wound.

He jumped up and raced out of the barn, knowing he

needed to put a bandage on it to stop the bleeding. *Sure hope no one sees me*, he thought. *Mom and Dad would be upset if they knew what I'd done.*

Mark entered the house and hurried down the hall to the bathroom. Then he opened the medicine chest and took out the box of bandages. The cut was bleeding so much that when he tried to put the bandage on, it wouldn't stick.

"Oh great! Now what am I gonna do?" Mark moaned.

Just then, Ike poked his head into the bathroom. "What's going on, Mark?" he asked, squinting his eyes. "Did you cut your thumb?"

Mark nodded, wishing he didn't have to explain. "I—I cut it with my pocketknife when I was tryin' to carve a little wagon from a hunk of wood I found in the barn."

Ike took hold of Mark's hand and studied the wound. "It's bleeding pretty badly, and I'll bet it's gonna need some stitches, too." He grabbed a clean towel and wrapped it around Mark's thumb. "Come on, little *bruder*. Let's go tell Mom and Dad, and hold the towel tight against the cut if you can. It might help slow down the bleeding."

Mark swallowed hard, struggling not to give in to his tears. He wished now he'd never found that old pocketknife!

CHAPTER 11

The Big Squeeze

"How's your thumb feeling now?" Mattie asked Mark as they sat at the table eating breakfast a week after Mark had cut his thumb with the pocketknife.

"It doesn't hurt much anymore, but my arm's still a little sore from the tetanus shot the doctor gave me," Mark said. "Sure wish I hadn't found that knife. It brought me nothin' but trouble."

"No," Dad said with a shake of his head. "The trouble came from you not asking your mamm and me if it was okay for you to keep the knife."

"Then, trying to carve something without being shown how only made it worse," Mom added.

Mark nodded soberly. "I know, and I'm sorry about that." He looked over at Dad. "Now that my thumb's feelin' better, would you show me how to carve?"

"I'd be happy to," Dad said. "Just let me know whenever you're ready—or even Ike could show you how it's done. He's pretty good at carving. After all, I taught him everything I know." Dad looked at Ike and winked. "In the meantime, though, I have some other things I need to be thinking about."

"Like what?" Calvin wanted to know.

Dad grinned and wiggled his bushy eyebrows. "Like making some freshly squeezed apple cider. After Ike and I are done chopping some firewood, I'm going to get out the old cider press and make sure it's clean and in good working order. Then this Saturday we'll spend the day making cider, and in the evening we'll have a hot dog and marshmallow roast around the bonfire."

Mattie smacked her lips. "Can we make some popcorn, too?"

"I don't see why not," Dad said. "That always goes good with fresh apple cider." He looked over at Mom and smiled. "Autumn is a great time of the year, isn't it?"

She gave a nod. "Jah, but then I enjoy all seasons— warm or cold."

Not me, Mattie thought. *I don't like the cold, snowy winter nearly as much as spring, summer, and fall.*

❖

On Saturday there was a lot of excitement at the Miller house as they all gathered around to watch Dad press the apples they'd picked a few days before into cider.

Mom had washed the apples first, of course, and she'd also cut out all the bad spots and bruises. Then the prepared apples were carefully dumped into the main box on the cider press. Inside the box was a grinder that had two small blades attached. One blade cracked the apples open, and the other blade shaved off the skins on the apples. After the apples had been cracked, shaved, and chopped, they fell into a slatted, bottomless tub. When the handle of the press was turned, the apple pulp was squeezed and packed down, making juice that trickled to the bottom of the press. After that, the juice flowed out into a clean container. Then Mom poured the juice into a piece of cheesecloth material to filter out the pulp and sediment. That made the amber-colored cider clean and pure when she poured it into clean, sterilized jars.

"How many apples does it take to make a gallon of fresh cider?" Mark asked.

"About twenty-six pounds of apples." Dad chuckled. "Now that's a big squeeze, wouldn't you say?"

Mark whistled. "Jah. That's a lot!"

Dad handed everyone a paper cup he'd filled with fresh cider. "Now take a drink and tell me what you think."

"It's appenditlich," Mattie said, licking her lips.

"That's right," Mom agreed. "And as it trickles down my throat, I'm thanking God for the variety of delicious foods He has provided for our enjoyment, as well as good health."

"I like fresh apple cider more than soda pop," Russell said. "And it's much better for you, too."

All heads bobbed in agreement.

"Mark and Mattie, I have a favor to ask," Mom said, placing one hand on each of the twins' shoulders.

"What's that?" they asked at the same time.

"We're running low on ketchup and mustard for the hot dogs we'll be roasting later this evening, and I'd like you to go to the store and get one bottle of each."

"Can't someone else go?" Mark asked. "I wanna stay here and watch Dad make more cider."

Mattie nodded. "Same goes for me."

"Well, I sure can't go," Mom said, "because I have

several more jars to wash and sterilize for the cider."

"And I can't go," Ike said. "I'm supposed to muck out the barn."

"Russell and I can't go to the store either," Calvin spoke up. "We need to haul all the apple peelings to the compost pile around back."

"So that leaves you two," Dad said, looking at Mark and Mattie. "If you ride your bicycle, it shouldn't take you long at all. And when you get back, you can watch me finish making the cider."

"Come into the house with me," Mom said. "I'll make out a list for you to take to the store and give you the money you'll need."

"Why do we need a list?" Mark questioned. "I thought we were just goin' for mustard and ketchup. I'm sure Mattie and I can remember those two items without havin' a list."

Mom smiled and patted the top of Mark's head. "I just thought of a few other things I could use as well."

"Will there be room for everything in our bicycle basket?" Mattie asked.

"I believe so," Mom said. "There aren't that many other things I need. I'll give you a canvas satchel to take along, and if there isn't room for everything in the basket, you can put the rest of the things in the satchel and ride home with it hanging from one of your handlebars."

"Okay, Mom," Mattie said.

Mark and Mattie followed Mom up to the house, and after she'd given them the list and money, she said, "If there's any money left over you can each buy a piece of candy."

"Danki, Mom," the twins both said.

❁

As Mark and Mattie pedaled their bicycle toward the store, they talked about the kind of candy they would buy.

"I want chocolate," Mark said.

"And I want strawberry," Mattie put in.

Mark chuckled. "I figured you would."

"Speaking of candy," Mattie said, "it was nice of our teacher to bring me a piece of strawberry-flavored candy the day she said she would."

"Jah. Anna Ruth's a real nice teacher," Mark agreed.

By the time the twins pulled up to the bicycle rack in front of the store, Mark's stomach was growling. "I'm hungerich," he told Mattie. "Mom gave us plenty of money, so I think I'll buy myself somethin' to eat."

"Mom said we're supposed to buy everything on her list, and if there's enough money left over, we can buy some candy," Mattie reminded him.

"I know, but if I don't eat somethin' right now I might not have enough strength left to pedal home. Besides, one piece of candy won't be enough." Mark tugged on Mattie's hand. "Let's go to the snack bar and see what we can find."

Mattie followed Mark into the store, and when they stepped up to the snack bar, Mark pointed to the tubs of ice cream. "Let's get a cone. I'll get chocolate, and you can have strawberry. Oh, and let's order some soda pop, too. After that long ride, I'm kinda thirsty."

Mattie looked hesitant at first, but she finally nodded.

After the twins got their cones and soda pop, they took a seat on a bench outside the store to eat their tasty treats.

"Yum. . . This is so good." Mattie swiped her tongue over the strawberry ice cream. "It's almost as good as the kind Dad makes."

Mark bobbed his head. "You're right about that."

After they finished eating their cones and drinking their soda pop, they went back inside and looked for the items they'd been sent there to get. They found everything on Mom's list, but when they got to the checkout counter and the clerk told them how much they owed, Mark knew they were in trouble. "We don't have enough money to pay for all this," he whispered to Mattie. "Now what are we gonna do?"

Her eyes widened. "I—I don't know. I really don't have a clue."

"Guess we're just gonna have to put some of this stuff back on the shelf. I can't think of anything else to do."

Mattie's eyebrows drew together. "What's Mom gonna say when we get home and don't have everything on her list?"

Mark shrugged his shoulders. "I don't know. She'll probably be mad, but if we get the ketchup and mustard, which we need for our meal tonight, maybe she won't be too upset. After all, those were the two most important items."

"True." Mattie smiled at the store clerk and said, "My brother and I will be right back." She scooped all their grocery items back into the cart and quickly pushed it away.

"Make sure you put everything back on the shelf where you found it," the clerk called after them.

"We will," Mark and Mattie said in unison.

After Mark added up the price of each thing on the list Mom had given them, they knew how much they could spend.

"Looks like we're gonna have to put the paper plates and plastic cups back on the shelf," Mark said. "Then we should have enough money to pay for the ketchup, mustard, potato chips, and hot dog buns."

"That should be okay," Mattie said. "We can use Mom's regular dishes to eat off tonight."

The twins went back to the register and paid for the things in their cart. Then they carried their sack out to the bike.

"Look, the sack fits just perfectly inside our basket," Mark said as he climbed on the front of the bicycle.

"Maybe it's a good thing we couldn't get everything on Mom's list, or it wouldn't have fit in the basket very well," Mattie said, positioning herself on the back of the bike. "I think it would have been harder to pedal if I'd had to put groceries in the satchel Mom gave us and then hang it over my handlebars. It could have bumped my knee."

Mark made no reply. He was almost sure that Mom would be upset when she found out they'd spent some of the money on ice cream and didn't have enough to buy all the things she'd asked them to get. He wished now that they could go back and do it over again, because if they could, he wouldn't have bought anything to eat or drink.

❁

"It's not fair that we have to do the dishes while everyone else is sitting around the bonfire, roasting marshmallows," Mattie complained as she reached into the drainer for another dish to dry.

"Mom thinks it's fair," Mark said, looking out the window above the sink, watching Dad put another marshmallow on Perry's stick. "Our punishment for spending some of the money she gave us on ice cream and soda pop, instead of keeping it for the things she wanted, is havin' to wash and dry the dishes and go without any dessert tonight."

"I wish Mom had given us more money and let us go back to the store for the rest of the items," Mattie said. "But no, she said she would take the horse and buggy and go to the store on Monday morning after we leave for school."

Mark sloshed the soapy sponge over one of the plates in the sink. "If we'd had enough money when we were at the store today to buy paper plates and plastic cups, we wouldn't have had to use Mom's dishes tonight."

"Jah, and we wouldn't be here in the kitchen right now," Mattie added. "We'd be out there eating tasty marshmallows and listening to one of Dad's stories about when he was a *yung bu*."

"I like hearing Dad tell about when he was a young boy," Mark said. "It makes me realize that he felt the same way I do sometimes."

Mattie nodded and reached for another plate to dry. "Sometimes I think Mom and Dad don't understand the way I feel about things, but then one of 'em tells something about the way it was when they were young, and then I think maybe they do know how I feel."

"Sometimes it's hard to realize that our folks were little once, like we are right now," Mark said.

"I know," Mattie agreed. "I can't really imagine them being kids, but I know they had to be." She giggled.

"When I grow up and have some kinner of my own, I'll tell 'em about lots of things I did as a boy." Mark reached over and tickled Mattie under her chin with his soapy finger. "I'll even tell 'em how I liked to tease my twin sister."

Mattie squinted her eyes and pushed his wet hand away. "You do and I'll tell 'em how you landed in stinky manure when you fell off the roof of the chicken coop."

Mark shook his head. "I didn't fall, Mattie. I floated off the roof when Dad's big umbrella lifted me into the air."

Mattie flapped her hand. "Thinkin' you could use that umbrella as a parachute was not very bright."

"I know that now, so don't rub it in."

"Sorry," Mattie said. "I was just makin' a point."

Mark grunted. "Well, one thing's for sure—I'll never do a crazy stunt like that again."

Mattie put the dishes she'd dried into the cupboard and closed the door. "Everyone's still sitting around the bonfire," she said, peeking out the kitchen window. "I sure do miss bein' out there with them tonight."

Mark's forehead wrinkled. "Jah, and now that we've finished the dishes, we have to go to bed."

"Mom said we need to learn a lesson," Mattie murmured. "I don't know about you, but I'll never use Mom's money to buy anything for myself at the store, ever again. At least not unless she tells me to."

Mark gave a nod. "Me neither."

CHAPTER 12

Purple Sheets

A week later, on a Friday night, Mattie tossed and turned in her bed, unable to find a comfortable position. For some reason she just couldn't sleep.

Maybe what I need is a glass of milk, she thought. Grandma Troyer had told Mattie once that whenever she drank a glass of warm milk before going to bed, it always put her to sleep. Of course, Mattie didn't think she would like warm milk, but a glass of cold milk would probably be just as good.

Quietly, Mattie slipped out of bed and tiptoed down the stairs. Everyone else was in bed, and she knew she'd have to be extra quiet or she might wake someone up.

When Mattie entered the kitchen, it was dark, so she turned on the battery-operated lantern Mom kept on the counter below the cupboards. Then Mattie took a clean glass from the cupboard and placed it on the table. She opened the refrigerator and was about to get out the milk when she spotted a blackberry pie—or what was left of one. Mom had made two pies yesterday, and they'd eaten one pie and part of the other for dessert last night. There was only one piece left of this pie, and boy, did it look good!

Mattie's stomach rumbled in protest, and her mouth watered just thinking about eating a piece of that delicious-looking hunk of blackberry pie.

Mattie wondered if Mom might be saving that piece for her or Dad's breakfast tomorrow. She stood several seconds, staring at the slice of pie, and finally decided to take it. After all, she was hungry, and the slice was sitting right there in front of her. . . .

Mattie placed the pie pan on the table and lifted the pie onto a napkin. After that, she poured herself a glass of milk. Then, afraid someone might hear her moving around in the kitchen, Mattie put the empty pie pan in the sink and turned off the lantern. Anxious to get upstairs to her room, she picked up the milk and pie then went quietly up the stairs.

Back in her room, Mattie set the milk and pie on the nightstand and sat down on her bed. Since she hadn't bothered to get a fork, she had to use her fingers to eat the pie. This worked fine until the blackberry juice started trickling down her fingers. Then, when she leaned over to lick it off, the rest of the pie she was about to eat slid off the napkin and onto her bed.

"Oh no!" Mattie gasped when she saw the bright purple stain all over the solid-white sheets. How was she going to explain this to Mom?

❧

"Mattie, I'm getting ready to do the laundry, so please bring your dirty clothes down now," Mom called up the stairs on Saturday morning.

Mattie, who'd been lying on her bed reading the book

about flowers, raced to the door and hollered, "I'll bring them down in a few minutes!"

"Oh, and don't forget to strip the sheets off your bed," Mom said. "Those need to be washed, too."

Mattie gulped. Until this very minute she'd forgotten about the blackberry stain on her sheets. After she'd tried unsuccessfully to get it off with a wet washcloth, she'd put a towel over the spot and slept on the other side of the bed. Now she had no choice but to admit what she'd done because Mom was sure to see that awful purple blotch before she put the sheets into the washing machine.

Mattie pulled aside the beautiful patchwork quilt on her bed. Thank goodness the quilt was still clean. Mattie didn't know what she would have done if the pie juice would have stained that, too. The sheet was bad enough!

Frowning at the purple stain, Mattie removed the sheets and pillowcases, placing them in the laundry basket along with all her dirty clothes. Then she picked up the basket and made her way slowly down the stairs.

"Oh, there you are," Mom said when she met Mattie at the bottom of the steps. "Everyone else has already put their dirty clothes in the basement, so I was just waiting on yours before I started the washer. Would you please carry your laundry basket down there, too?"

"Uh, Mom. . .there's something I need to tell you."

"Can it wait a bit, Mattie? I really want to get the batch of clothes washed so I can hang them on the line to dry in case it decides to rain. There's a good breeze blowing this morning, and everything should dry fairly fast, I expect."

"Okay." Mattie hauled the basket down to the basement.

"You can go back to whatever you were doing now,"

Mom said when she joined Mattie there by the washer.

Mattie shook her head. "I—I can't, Mom. Not till I tell ya something."

"Let me get this first load into the washing machine, and then you can tell me whatever you like." Mom knelt on the floor and lifted Mattie's sheets out of the basket. She'd just started putting them into the washer when she halted. "Ach, what's this?" she asked, pointing to the ugly purple stain.

Mattie swallowed hard. "That's what I've been tryin' to tell ya."

Mom squinted and rubbed the bridge of her nose. "I'd like to hear what you know about this horrible-looking stain on your *leinduch*."

Mattie quickly explained how she'd gotten out of bed last night, taken the piece of blackberry pie, and accidentally dropped it on her sheet. "I'm sorry, Mom," she said, tears welling in her eyes. "I know it was wrong and selfish of me to take the last piece. I—I didn't mean to drop it, either. I was so hungerich last night, my stomach wouldn't stop growling, and when I saw that last piece of pie, I just had to have it."

Mom pursed her lips. "You should know better than to help yourself to something without asking, and I've told you many times that I don't want you taking food to your room unless I've given my permission."

"I know, and I promise never to do it again."

Mom pulled Mattie into her arms and gave her a hug. "I forgive you, Mattie, but you must learn a lesson from your disobedience."

Mattie sniffed and swiped at the tears rolling down her cheeks. "Are you gonna give me a *bletsching*?"

Mom shook her head. "No, I'm not going to spank you, but after I've washed the clothes, it will be your job to hang them on the line to dry. Then later this afternoon, I'll have some extra chores for you to do."

Mattie knew she'd done wrong and deserved to be punished, so she didn't give a word of protest. "I'll go outside and wait on the porch," she told Mom. "When the first batch of clothes is done, I'll be ready to hang them out to dry."

❧

"How'd you like to take turns pullin' each other in our little red wagon?" Mark called when he spotted Mattie standing on a wooden stool, hanging the laundry on the clothesline.

"I can't right now," Mattie said. "I have to finish doin' this."

Mark sprinted over to the clothesline. "How 'bout when you're done?"

"Maybe, but that won't be for a while yet." She motioned to the clothes in the basket. "As you can see, I still have a lot of things left to hang."

Mark flopped down on the grass beside the basket. "I'll wait till you're finished."

"Why don't you help?" Mattie suggested. "That way I can get done a lot quicker."

Mark shook his head. "I'd rather not."

"How come?"

" 'Cause men don't hang clothes on the line."

Mattie snickered. "You're not a *mann*, Mark. You're still a bu."

"Maybe so, but I'm growing older every day, and pretty soon I'll be a man."

Mattie said nothing—just picked up a green towel and hung it on the line.

"Wanna play a little game?" he asked.

"No. Can't you see that I'm busy?"

"This is the kind of game you can play while you work. It's a question and answer game."

She bent to pick up another towel. "What kinds of questions?"

"Bible questions." Mark plucked a blade of grass and stuck it between his teeth. "If you can answer all five of my questions, I'll help you hang up the rest of the clothes."

"Okay," Mattie agreed. "That sounds good to me. What's the first question?"

"There was a man in the Bible who used a stone for a pillow. Do you know his name?"

"Hmm. . ." Mattie rubbed her chin. "I remember Dad reading that Bible story to us once. Let's see now. . .was it Jacob?"

Mark nodded. He couldn't believe Mattie remembered that story. Maybe she would do better at this game than he thought.

"What's the next question?" Mattie asked.

"Who was the oldest man in the Bible, and how long did he live?"

Mattie tipped her head and squinted her eyes, like she was thinking real hard. "Let's see now. . .was it Noah?"

"Nope. The man's name was Methuselah, and he lived 969 years."

Mattie's mouth dropped open. "Wow! He must have

had a very long beard!"

Mark chuckled. "Jah, I'll bet it was even longer than Grandpa Troyer's and Grandpa Miller's beards; and theirs come way down here." He placed his hand in the middle of his chest.

"You're right—both of our grandpas have pretty long beards."

"Are you ready for the next question?" Mark asked.

Mattie shook her head. "There's no point in me trying to answer another question."

"How come?"

"I already missed one answer, and you said if I got them all correct you'd help me finish hanging the laundry."

Mark shrugged his shoulders. "Guess you're right, but you could still try to answer the other three questions."

"Huh-uh."

"Pl–e–a–s–e. . ."

Mattie picked up another towel and snapped it in front of Mark's face. "I'm done with your game!"

He grinned. *I'll bet if I keep asking her questions she'll answer.* "What is the shortest verse in the Bible?"

"I have no idea."

"It's just two words."

"I don't know," Mattie said.

" 'Jesus wept.' It's found in John 11:35."

"That is a short verse."

Mark cleared his throat real loud. "Last question: What is the longest word in the Bible?"

"You may as well tell me 'cause I have no idea at all," Mattie said, clipping a pair of Dad's trousers to the line.

"Are you ready for this?"

"Jah."

"The longest word in the Bible is Maher-Shalal-Hash-Baz. It's a name that was given to a *boppli*."

"What a strange name for a baby," Mattie said.

"I know, but not all Bible names are strange." Mark smiled. "My name is in the Bible. It's in the New Testament, in fact."

Mattie nodded. "Jah, the Book of Mark."

"That's right." Mark pointed to the laundry basket, which was empty. "Can I get out the wagon now?"

"Sure," Mattie said, "but only if I get to ride in it first."

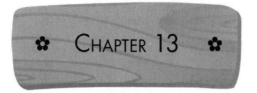

CHAPTER 13

Consequences

"Don't go so fast!" Mattie hollered as Mark pulled the wagon up the driveway. "You're makin' me bounce too much!"

"Just hang on and enjoy the ride," Mark called over his shoulder.

Mattie gripped the sides of the wagon a little tighter. Every time it hit a bump, her stomach flew up, just like it did when she got the swing in their backyard going too high. It was fun being pulled in the wagon, though.

"Okay, it's my turn to ride now." Mark stopped the wagon near the barn and motioned for Mattie to get out.

Mattie frowned. "Already? I didn't get a very long turn."

"Jah, you did," he said. "I pulled you up and down the driveway four times, and now you have to do the same for me."

"Oh, all right." Mattie climbed out of the wagon, and Mark took her place. Then she grabbed hold of the handle, turned the wagon around, and started down the driveway.

"Go faster, Mattie!" Mark shouted. "Run, schnell!"

"I'm going as quickly as I can," Mattie panted, trying to keep ahead of the wagon before it bumped into her.

Every time the wagon hit a bump, Mark laughed and hollered, "More! More! Schnell, Mattie!"

By the time Mattie had pulled Mark up and down the driveway four times, she was worn out. "Whew! I need to rest awhile," she said, flopping down on the grass.

"You can rest in the wagon while I'm pulling you," Mark said.

She shook her head. "It's kind of hard to rest when the wagon is jigglin' my tummy and shakin' my teeth."

Mark chuckled. "But that's what makes riding in the wagon so much fun, don't you think?"

"Jah, but I need to rest a bit before I go for another ride."

"Okay." Mark took a seat on the lawn beside Mattie and leaned his head back to look at the sky. Mattie figured he was probably studying the clouds.

"The puffy clouds look like giant pillows, don't they?" Mark asked. He pointed toward the nearby oak tree. "Hey, look! A bunch of blue jays just landed in that tree."

She smiled and closed her eyes. "Jah. If I had my pillow with me right now, I'd take a nap, and those birds could sing me to sleep."

Mark tickled her under the chin.

"Absatz!" she said, pushing his hand away. "If you don't stop, I'll tickle your feet."

"You can't; I'm wearin' my boots today, and you'd have a hard time gettin' them off."

"I could call Russell or Calvin to help me," she said in a teasing tone.

"Better not, or I'll run and hide."

Mattie giggled. "Then don't tickle me anymore."

"All right, I won't," Mark said, still staring up at the clouds. "I sure do miss Ike not bein' around as much as he used to be, don't you?"

"I guess so," Mattie answered. "But then Ike used to do more things with you, like fishing and other boy stuff."

"I know, but I never thought Ike would quit doin' the things we used to do together just so he could take some girl for a ride in his buggy or go to singings and such."

"You must be talking about Catherine," Mattie said.

"Jah."

"You shouldn't talk about her like that. I think she's real nice."

"Humph!" Mark didn't have much to say about that. It wasn't right that Catherine had pushed her way in. At least, that's how Mark saw it. "She's monopolizing all of Ike's time these days."

"Mon-opo-lizing?"

"Jah. It means she's takin' up all of Ike's free time that he used to spend with me," Mark explained.

"Oh Mark, you're just actin' silly. Someday you'll be doing that, too." Mattie smiled. "Especially if you meet the right *maedel*."

"Not me. Don't care if I ever meet the right girl." Mark quickly shook his head. "No way, not me!"

"You know, Ike's not just with Catherine. They're usually with a group of friends their own age, just like you are with your friends," Mattie said in defense of her oldest brother.

"Well, I still don't like it."

Just then, Perry came running out of the house and jumped into the wagon. "I wanna *faahre*!" he hollered.

"You're not going for a ride today," Mark said with a shake of his head. "This is Mattie's and my wagon."

Perry's lower lip protruded. "I wanna faahre!"

"Why don't you go back in the house and find something else to do?" Mattie said. She was already tired from pulling Mark in the wagon and didn't want to do it for Perry now, too.

Perry's forehead wrinkled, and tears welled in his eyes. "I'm tellin' Mom on you."

Before either Mattie or Mark had a chance to respond, he hopped out of the wagon and raced to the house. A few minutes later, he returned, and Mom was with him.

"What's this I hear about you not letting your little bruder take a ride in the wagon?" she asked, looking first at Mattie and then Mark.

"It's our wagon, and Mattie and I are takin' turns pulling each other up and down the driveway," Mark said.

"That's fine, but you should share. Now, is there any reason why you can't give Perry a ride?"

Mattie shook her head. Mark did the same. Mattie knew if they didn't let Perry take a ride, Mom would probably make them put the wagon away.

❧

After Mom went back in the house, Perry climbed into the wagon again. "I'm ready for my ride," he said, grinning up at Mark.

Mark leaned close to Mattie and whispered in her ear, "Maybe if we give Perry a wild enough ride, he won't like it and will go back inside. Then we can have the wagon all to ourselves again."

"That might work," Mattie agreed. "I'll pull, and you can push. That will make the wagon go even faster."

"Good idea," Mark said.

Mattie grabbed hold of the handle, and Mark put his hands on the back of the wagon. "Alright, Perry!" he shouted. "Here we go!"

Perry squealed with laughter as the wagon rolled along the driveway and then zigzagged back and forth through the grass. He seemed to be having a great time and wasn't the least bit afraid. Mark figured they might be stuck pulling their little brother all over the yard for the rest of the day— or at least until Mom called them in for lunch.

"Pull the wagon over there," Mark called to Mattie as he pointed to some big bumps along the edge of the driveway.

"Okay." Mattie pulled the wagon in that direction.

"Now run as fast as you can!"

Mattie did as Mark said, and while she pulled, he pushed as hard as he could. They were going so fast and making so much racket, the blue jays that had flown into the nearby tree flew back out in every direction to get away from the loud noise. The wagon picked up speed, hit one of the bumps, and—*whoomp!*—Perry bounced right out.

"Yeow!" he hollered, and then he started to sob while holding his head.

"Oh no, I think he's hurt!" Mattie dropped the handle of the wagon and raced to Perry's side. Mark did the same.

Sure enough, there was a gash on Perry's forehead, and it was bleeding.

"Go get Mom!" Mattie shouted. "Schnell!"

✿

Mark paced the floors while Mattie kept Ada occupied. It had been more than two hours since Mom and Dad took Perry to the hospital to have his forehead looked at. What could be taking them so long? Mark hoped his little brother wasn't seriously hurt.

"You're gonna wear a hole in your boots if you don't stop pacin' back and forth like that," Russell called from across the room where he sat reading a book.

"I can't help it. I'm worried about Perry."

Mattie left Ada and joined Mark as he walked back and forth. "It's our fault Perry fell out of the wagon. We shouldn't have gone so fast and taken him over those bumps."

"I know," Mark agreed. "But I didn't think he'd get hurt. I just wanted to scare him a bit so he'd go back in the house."

"Remember when Grandpa said we'd have a bumpy ride ahead if we didn't stop being selfish?"

Mark nodded. "Guess our little bruder's the one who got the bumpy ride, but it wouldn't have happened if we hadn't been so selfish."

"Jah. We should have given him a nice easy ride instead of trying to scare him," Mattie said.

Mark heard the rumble of a vehicle coming up the driveway, so he stopped pacing and hurried over to the window. "It's Mom, Dad, and Perry! Their driver just pulled in," he announced.

Mattie raced to the front door and pulled it open. Then both she and Mark stepped onto the porch.

"How's Perry doing?" Mark called as his parents and little brother approached the house.

"His knees are scraped up, and the doctor put four stitches in Perry's forehead, but he's going to be okay," Mom replied.

Dad looked sternly at the twins. "I'd like to know one thing. How come you were pulling Perry so fast in the wagon that he fell out?"

Mark dropped his gaze. It was hard for him to look at Dad when he knew he'd done something wrong. "We didn't mean for Perry to fall out. We just wanted to scare him a little so he wouldn't want to ride in the wagon anymore and we could have it all to ourselves."

"I see. So because of your selfishness, your little brother has a nasty gash on his forehead."

"I'm sorry," Mark and Mattie said at the same time. "We won't ever do anything like that again."

"I should hope not," Mom said. "A selfish attitude isn't pleasing to God."

"I know, and we've learned a good lesson," Mark said.

Mattie nodded in agreement.

"I'm glad to hear that," Dad said. "But your actions deserve some kind of punishment, don't you think?"

"Jah," Mark and Mattie both gave a quick nod. It seemed like lately, more so than ever, they'd been getting punished a lot and trying to remember the lessons they'd learned from all their wrongdoings.

Dad turned and motioned to the wagon, still sitting in the yard. "The wagon will be put in the barn, and neither of you will be allowed to ride in it for two weeks."

Two weeks seemed like an awfully long time, but Mark

didn't argue with Dad. Instead he smiled and said, "The next time Perry or Ada wants to play with something of mine, I'm gonna share."

"Me, too," Mattie put in. "I don't want any more bumpy rides."

CHAPTER 14

Discoveries

For the next two weeks, Mark and Mattie remembered not to be selfish and to think about others rather than themselves. But that all changed one Saturday morning when Mom came into the living room where Mark and Mattie sat at a small table, working on a puzzle together.

"I'm taking Perry and Ada, and we're going over to see Freda Hostetler this morning," Mom announced. "I thought maybe you two would like to come along."

Mark shook his head. "I'd rather stay here and work on the puzzle Mattie and I have started."

"What about you, Mattie?" Mom asked. "Wouldn't you like to see Freda?"

"I don't think so, Mom. I wanna finish this puzzle today."

"You know, children," Mom said, "Freda lives alone and gets lonely sometimes. I'm sure she would enjoy your company."

"Maybe some other time," Mark said. "We don't want to go over there today."

Mom's brows furrowed; she really looked disappointed. "All right then. I won't force you to go." She called Perry and Ada to come, and they all went out the door.

"Maybe we should have gone with them," Mattie said. "Freda always gives us something whenever we stop by her house to visit after school."

Mark nodded. "That's true. Once she gave me a little cage to catch tadpoles in."

"She gave me some flowers she'd dried so I could make a bookmark," Mattie said. "Oh, and she usually gives us a snack to eat."

"You're right, and to tell ya the truth, that's the real reason I ever go there. I mean, it's not like Freda has any kinner for us to play with. She's old, and her grandkids live in another state." Mark turned his hands over so his palms were straight up. "I just didn't feel like goin' there today."

"Me neither," Mattie agreed. "I'd much rather be here."

"Let's get back to work on the puzzle now," Mark said. "If we work fast, maybe we can get it put together before Mom, Ada, and Perry get home."

"I can't work fast on the puzzle," Mattie said. "Looking for the right pieces that will fit together takes time. Besides, this puzzle is harder than most." Mattie motioned to the picture on the box. It was of a big red barn with lots of puffy clouds in the sky, and they all looked the same.

"It's not hard for me." Mark picked up an end piece and slipped it right in place.

Mattie wrinkled her nose. "Hey! I was just gonna pick that one up."

"Guess we think alike." Mark snickered. "At least on some things, anyway."

"There are lots of things we don't think the same

way about," Mattie said, leaning closer to the puzzle and squinting her eyes.

"You're right, and I know one thing we don't agree on."

"What's that?"

"I can't wait for winter 'cause I really like the *schnee*, but I know that you don't care much for snow."

Mattie nodded. "But I do think it's fun when we get to build a snowman or go sledding."

"I like that, too," Mark said. "Oh, and I always enjoy going ice-skating."

"Not me," Mattie said with a shake of her head. "I worry that the ice might be too thin and I'll fall through and drown in that chilly cold water."

"Well, you can worry about that when winter comes. Right now we need to concentrate on findin' the right pieces to fit into this puzzle."

❀

For the next hour, the twins worked on the puzzle and teased each other about who would get to put in the very last piece.

As the puzzle neared completion, Mark started picking up pieces lickety-split and then putting them in the proper place. Just when Mattie would reach for a piece of the puzzle, Mark would quickly grab it up.

It's not fair. He's not even giving me a chance to put any in, Mattie fumed. Then an idea popped into her head. As Mark was busy putting another puzzle piece in place, she grabbed the nearest piece to her, closed her fist around it, and placed her hand in her lap. Then she sat and watched as Mark put in one piece after another until there was just one empty space left.

Mark's brows furrowed as he studied the puzzle and looked all around and even under the table. "Now that's sure strange," he muttered.

"What's strange?"

"The last piece is missing."

"No it's not. I have it right here." Mattie, feeling quite pleased with herself, slipped the last piece in place and clapped her hands. "There, the puzzle's all done!"

The skin around Mark's eyes crinkled as he stared hard at Mattie. "You had that piece the whole time, didn't you?"

She shook her head. "Not the whole time. I just picked it up a few minutes ago."

"That's not fair. You cheated." Mark's eyes narrowed.

"Well, if I hadn't picked it up, you probably would have."

"Maybe, but not till it was time to put the last piece in place. You took it before it was time."

Mattie was about to say more, but their conversation was interrupted when Mom, Perry, and Ada came in the door.

"We had a nice time at Freda's," Mom said, "but she was really disappointed that you two didn't come see her today. She even made your favorite ginger cookies, thinking you two would be coming with me and the little ones."

Mattie looked at Mark, and Mark looked at Mattie. From the sad expression she saw on his face, she figured he felt as bad as she did about not going to see Freda.

"It was selfish of us to stay home," Mattie said.

"That's right," Mark agreed. He looked up at Mom and said, "If it's okay with you, Mattie and I can stop by to see Freda Monday afternoon on our way home from school."

Mom smiled and gave the twins' shoulders a gentle squeeze. "It's just fine with me."

❁

Monday afternoon, as the twins pedaled their bike home from school, Mark remembered that they'd agreed to stop by Freda Hostetler's place.

"Where are you going?" Mattie asked as Mark turned onto the road where Freda lived.

"We're stoppin' by Freda's house. Did you forget?"

"Oh that's right. I wonder what she'll give us today."

"Whatever it is, I don't think we should take it," Mark called over his shoulder.

"How come?"

"Remember on Saturday, how we talked about being selfish, and how the main reason we've always gone to see Freda is because she gives us things?"

"Jah, now I remember. Guess if she offers to give us something today, we'd better say no."

Mark smiled. He was glad he and Mattie were in agreement on this. It wouldn't do for one of them to take whatever Freda gave and the other one to turn it down.

When they entered Freda's yard, they parked the bike by her porch and sprinted up the stairs. Mark knocked once on the door and was about to knock again when Freda opened it and said, "It's nice to see you, Mark and Mattie, but I'm sorry, I won't be able to visit with you today."

"How come?" Mattie asked.

"There's an English family who lives down the road a ways, and last night their house caught fire." Freda slowly shook her head, and her brown eyes looked so sad. "That poor family lost everything they owned."

"That's *baremlich*!" Mattie exclaimed.

"It sure is terrible," Mark put in. "Was anyone in the family hurt?"

"No," said Freda. "They weren't at home when the fire started, so that was a good thing."

"I'm surprised we didn't hear about this sooner." Mark looked over at Mattie and noticed how sad she looked. "Anna Ruth must not know about it either, or she would have said somethin' during school today, don't ya think?"

Mattie gave a slow nod.

"The family is staying with some other English neighbors right now," Freda said. "And I've been busy all day gathering up some things to give them."

"We should go home and tell Mom and Dad about this," Mark said. "I'm sure they'll want to help that family, too."

"Before you go, would you like something to eat?" Freda asked. "I baked some more cookies today, and you can take them with you."

"No thanks," Mark said. "We didn't come here to get anything. We just came by to say hi and see how you're doing."

Freda smiled. "I appreciate that."

"We'll come by to visit you some other day," Mattie said before they climbed onto their bike and rode away.

✿

That evening during supper, Mark and Mattie told their family about the English family whose house had burned down.

"I heard about that," Dad said. "Someone came into the wood shop today and told me and Ike the news."

"I can't imagine what it must be like to lose your house and everything you own," Mom said. "I think we need to do something to help that family."

Dad nodded. "I agree. In fact, I spoke to a few people in our community today, and we're going to help build the family a new house."

"You can count on my help," Ike said.

Russell and Calvin said they would help, too.

"What can Mattie and I do?" Mark wanted to know.

"Well, some in our community are going to gather up things that the family will need in their new home," Dad said. He looked at the twins and smiled. "What I think the two of you can do is donate a few of your toys."

"Sure, we can do that," Mattie was quick to say. "I'm sure I can find several things to give away."

"Me, too," Mark said with a nod. "As soon as supper's over, I'll go upstairs to my room and pick out some toys."

Mark ate everything on his plate. As soon as Dad said he could be excused, he hurried upstairs.

Since Mark's toys were scattered all over his room, he had to spend several minutes looking. *Here's something I could give away, and I wouldn't even miss it*, Mark thought, picking up his old yo-yo.

He glanced around and spotted the baseball mitt his

friend John had given him as a birthday present a few
months ago. Since Mark didn't like playing ball and had
never used the mitt, he'd have no problem giving it up.
However, Mark figured it might hurt John's feelings if he
gave his gift away.

Tap! Tap! Tap!

Mark looked at the door. "Who is it?" he called.

"It's me—Mattie. Can I come in?"

"Jah, sure."

Mattie stepped into the room. In one hand she held a
stuffed bear with a missing ear. In her other hand was a
pair of old ice skates that used to be Mom's when she was
a girl.

"I found these to give to the kinner who lost their toys
in the fire," Mattie said. "What'd you find, Mark?"

Mark motioned to the baseball mitt and yo-yo that
he'd placed on his bed. "Don't think I'd miss either of
these one little bit, but I can't give John's present away, so
I need to come up with somethin' else, I guess."

"I won't miss the things I chose either." Mattie sighed
as she sat on the end of Mark's bed. "Only thing is, I don't
feel good about it."

Mark tipped his head. "You don't feel good about
giving some of your toys to the kids who lost all theirs?"

"It's not that. I just don't feel good about the things I
chose because they're things I don't want anymore."

Mark's fingers made little circles on his forehead as he
thought things through. "To tell ya the truth, I don't feel
good about what I chose either. I think what we need to
do is give those kids something nice—something we really
like ourselves."

"I agree." Mattie leaped to her feet. "I know what I can give."

"What's that?" Mark asked.

"I'll give away one of my nicest dolls. Not the one my friend Stella gave me for my birthday, though. That might hurt Stella's feelings. But I have other dolls that are really nice, so I'll give up one of those." Mattie smiled. "Think I'll also give away some of my books or one of my favorite board games."

"Let's see now. . . I know!" Mark clapped his hands together. "I'll give the pocketknife I found a few weeks ago and also some of my best marbles. I have a game that I could give away, too."

"I feel good about giving away some of our favorite things," Mattie said.

"Jah. The pocketknife has a nice inscription etched into the blade that reads: 'Soar high, like an Eagle.' That might help 'em to feel hopeful."

"I'm sure it will," Mattie agreed.

Mark had a good feeling in his heart. It was much better to give than receive.

❖

A week later, on a Friday afternoon, Mattie was up at the entrance to their driveway because she'd spotted a few more wildflowers blooming on her way home from school. Ironweed was a hardy plant, and it was about the only thing still blooming this time of year. After Mattie had picked a few stems, she went over to the empty produce stand to sit and work on the flowers before she gave them to Mom. The air had turned cooler recently, and now it really felt like winter was on its way. Even though it was sunny today, the warmth didn't seem to be breaking through as it had only a few short weeks ago.

Mattie pulled the collar of her jacket up around her neck as she took a few leaves off the lower part of the flower stems and snapped off the bottoms. She'd seen Mom do that the last time she'd surprised her with a bouquet of wildflowers. Soon it would be Thanksgiving, but Mattie doubted there'd be any flowers left by then, so she was glad she'd noticed these ironweeds that were still blooming.

As she worked on the wildflowers, something shiny caught her eye, lying over by their mailbox. She laid the flowers down and walked over to the object. When she discovered what it was, she smiled and reached down and put it in her apron pocket.

❁

That evening after silent prayer, Mom and Dad thanked everyone for the help they'd given to the English family who'd lost their home to the fire. The older boys had given all their free time to help with rebuilding the house, and Mark and Mattie were unselfish in giving up their favorite toys to the children who'd lost all of theirs.

"Oh, and Mattie, I want to thank you again for providing our beautiful centerpiece for the table this evening," Mom said, smiling at Mattie.

"Ern weed," little Ada spoke up.

The whole family smiled, and Mattie was amazed that her little sister actually remembered the name of the flower she'd picked, even if she couldn't say the word exactly right.

"You're right, Ada. That's *ironweed.*" If she'd been sitting near Ada, Mattie would have tweaked her little nose. Ada was so cute, trying to sound all grown up.

Mom reached over and tugged gently on one of Ada's flaming red braids. "It seems we may have another girl in the family who loves flowers."

Everyone smiled at Ada while she giggled and pointed at the flowers.

"Can I say something?" Mark asked in a serious tone.

"Of course you can," Dad answered with a nod of his head.

The rest of the family looked at Mark, as though curious and wondering what he was about to say. It wasn't like Mark to ask when he wanted to say something. He usually just spoke right up and said whatever was on his mind.

"Actually, I have two things," Mark stated. "First, I've been studyin' up on the Heimlich maneuver. That's what saved Grandma Miller's life, ya know—the day she choked on the hot dog. I think it'd be wise if we all learned how to do the maneuver, in case we ever need to use it. Now, after reading all about it, I think I could do it."

"First aid is a good thing to learn," Dad agreed, "because you never know when you might have to use it."

"If it wouldn't have been for that guy Tony, who knows what could have happened to Grandma?" Mattie added.

"Okay now, I have somethin' else to say," Mark announced, his face turning red.

"What is it, son?" Mom asked.

"I just wanna say that it felt really good to give up somethin' of mine that I really liked but could do without to make someone else happy." Mark's face turned redder. "I don't really miss that pocketknife I found along the road or the marbles I gave up either. Those can be replaced one day, I guess."

Mattie smiled, feeling pretty good herself. "That English family lost everything, but they still have each other, and that's what's most important."

"You're so right, Mattie," Dad said. "God blessed those people in a special way. Objects can be replaced, but family can't."

All heads bobbed in agreement.

"I'm hungerich," Perry suddenly spoke up.

"Before we eat, I have a little surprise for Mark," Mattie said. "Now, close your eyes and hold out your hand."

Mark did as Mattie asked.

Placing the object in Mark's hand and closing his fingers around it, Mattie said, "You can open your eyes now."

Mark's eyes popped open, and he stared at his hand with a look of surprise. Did he realize what she'd put in there?

"Well, what is it?" Russell asked.

"Jah. Don't keep us in suspense any longer!" Ike said with a chuckle.

Mattie held her breath as she watched Mark slowly open his fingers and stare at what she had placed in his hand.

"My glicker!" Mark squealed. He was obviously very pleased that his prized marble had been found. "Where did you find it, Mattie?"

"Well, this afternoon after I picked those flowers for Mom and went over to the produce stand to fix 'em up,

I noticed something shiny lying by the mailbox. When I went to take a closer look, I couldn't believe what I discovered. There it was—just like that—your favorite glicker—the one you'd lost in that pile of leaves."

Mark grinned and gave Mattie a quick hug. "Danki, Mattie. Getting my favorite glicker back just made my day."

Mattie couldn't get over how good it felt to surprise her twin brother. It was almost like she were receiving the surprise instead of Mark.

"I don't know about you, Alice," Dad said, looking at Mom, "but I'm sure pleased with our kinner. God has rewarded us over and over again, and tonight is just another example of that."

"Those are my exact thoughts as well, Willard," Mom said, smiling widely. "I'm so happy to see the joy our children have experienced in learning what it's like to be generous and not selfish."

"Mattie," Ike said, "I'll bet you feel just as rewarded, surprising Mark with his marble, as he did receiving it."

All Mattie could do was to nod her head because it was too hard to speak around the lump in her throat.

Mark reached over and squeezed Mattie's hand. "I'm glad I have a twin sister like you."

"What about me? I haven't done nothin'," Perry said with a pout.

"Oh, I wouldn't say that, son." Dad patted Perry's shoulder. "Look how brave you were when you had to have stitches. You sat there, being brave again, when the doctor removed them the following week. And don't forget how you looked after Ada when your mamm was busy cooking food to share with the English family who'd lost everything."

"That's right," Mom agreed. "We all played an important part in helping the people who went through such a tragic event. No matter what the role was, we did it as a family to help another family in need."

That seemed to pacify their little brother, and the whole family laughed when Perry said, "Okay, now, would somebody please pass the smashed taters?"

ABOUT THE AUTHOR

WANDA E. BRUNSTETTER is a bestselling author who enjoys writing historical, as well as Amish-themed novels. Descended from Anabaptists herself, Wanda became fascinated with the Plain People when she married her husband, Richard, who grew up in a Mennonite church in Pennsylvania. Wanda and her husband live in Washington State. They have two grown children and six grandchildren. Wanda and Richard often travel the country, visiting their many Amish friends and gathering further information about the Amish way of life. In her spare time, Wanda enjoys photography, ventriloquism, gardening, reading, stamping, and having fun with her family. Visit Wanda's Website at www.wandabrunstetter.com and feel free to e-mail her at wanda@wandabrunstetter.com.

Rachel Yoder—
Always Trouble Somewhere!

Join Rachel Yoder on a series of adventures with these 4-in-1 story collections written by bestselling author of Amish fiction Wanda E. Brunstetter. Whether Rachel is bringing frogs to church, chasing ornery roosters, or taking wild buggy rides, girls will encounter a lovable character who finds trouble nipping at her bare-footed heels at every turn!

Look Out, Lancaster County!

Growing Up in Lancaster County

Available wherever books are sold.